Series

The Blood Rite Saga

The Blood Empire: Episode One

The Blood Princess: Episode One

The Blood Princess: Episode Two

The Blood Princess: Episode Three

The Blood Princess: Episode Four

The Blood Princess: Episode Five

The Chronicles of Gandos

The Sword of Light

The Aurora Chronicles

Child of Winter

Lake of Prophecy

Taste of Battle

Heart of Will

Spirits of Arktika

The Raine Michelson Files

Angel's Poison

Demon's Match

Satan's Torment

Devil's Advocate

Lucifer's Wake

Mischief Miles Investigations

A Familiar Scent

Breaking and Entering

Like Father, Like Son

Too Close For Comfort

Mr. Right or Mr. Wrong

Everscape Online

Traitor of Golden Blaze

Queen of Ragnarok

Champion of Everscape

Britney Allen: The London Crime Syndicate

Blood of Babes: The Slasher Files

Standalone

Lost in Space

The Lone Survivor

Mr. Buddy Bot

Evelyn

LIKE FATHER, LIKE SON

MISCHIEF MILES INVESTIGATIONS

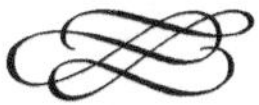

DYLAN KEEFER

I dedicate this book to my friends and family who have always supported in my dream of being a professional author.

— DYLAN KEEFER

USA Today Bestselling Author

DYLAN KEEFER

CHAPTER 1

CITY FARE

Her head was pounding. It hurt so much that she wanted to end the suffering by smashing her head against the window. She glanced up. It was too far away. The way he had tied her up made it almost impossible to move. Plus, he thought she was still unconscious. His voice carried through the car as he sang along to some song she had never heard of. She tried to feel her fingers. Her legs weren't bound; maybe if she could free her hands, she could escape.

Demetria wasn't exactly sure what had happened. She remembered the drink.

"Stop it," Arizona laughed as she pulled the straw out of Demetria's mouth. "Demi, you always do that. You always say you aren't hungry or thirsty, and then you take half my stuff."

"Well, I'm not hungry or thirsty until you get something. Plus, sharing is caring."

Arizona frowned at the little soda that was left.

"You're just lucky I'm a caring person."

"Do we have to go back to school?" Demi whined as she looked at her phone. "I have a test today."

"And you're going to have to make it up at some point. You might as well fail it now." Arizona joked. "Besides, I feel bad we didn't invite any of the others."

"Why? It's not like we didn't invite them to a party or something. It was lunch, and we don't always have to be around the others." Arizona nodded slowly, but the guilt was still on her face. Demi rolled her eyes. "You have too good of a heart, you know it."

"And you love me for it," Arizona said as she smiled brightly. "Come on, the bus station is a couple of blocks this way."

"Let's just grab a taxi," Demi said stepping towards the curb and raising her hand.

"Um, let's not," her friend grimaced. "You know what's going on in the news, right. Taxi kidnappings?"

"We're not going to get kidnapped," Demi said. "I've been taking taxis since those things started. We'll be fine."

A cab pulled up, and the two girls climbed inside. Arizona stared at the driver. He didn't look creepy. He didn't even make eye contact with them.

"Where to?"

"Adonis Prep school," Demi directed. She received an

elbow from Arizona who couldn't believe her friend had given out their exact school. Demi waved her off.

The cab driver began to pull out into traffic. Demi sighed and leaned her head against Arizona's shoulder.

"How'd it go with your parents, by the way?" Arizona asked.

"Didn't tell them."

She groaned.

"Demi, you've got to soon. They're going to find out one way or another."

Ari ran her fingers through her friend's hair, but her mind started to focus on something else. She knew the way back to school from where they were. They were heading in the directions that she was familiar with. In fact, they were heading away from the school. She slumped in her seat.

"Demi, he's not taking us back to school." Her voice was shaky as she kept her eyes on the cab driver.

"What are you talking about?" Demi mimicked her whisper.

"He's taking us somewhere. We need to get out of this car."

For the first time, the driver's eyes looked back at them through the rear view mirror. They were cold and dark. Even Demi felt it. She swallowed hard as she grabbed Arizona's hand.

"You girls skip school today?"

"Nope," Arizona said quickly with a shaky voice. "Just

had to, um, run an errand for our teacher. She's expecting us back any moment."

The driver raised an eyebrow. Demi closed her eyes. Arizona wasn't a good liar. That's why she always executed plans. She looked out of the window. Their best bet was to run out of the car as soon as they got to the next light. Hopefully, there was enough people around that they could get away. She squeezed Arizona's hand and didn't let go. There was a red light coming up. Once he stopped, they would be free to run. *Almost there.* Suddenly, the car jerked to the side sending Arizona into the side of the car, and Demi into her. The car zoomed down a lone alley. Before they could get their wits about them and before the car even stopped, the driver was out. Demi felt herself being dragged out by her hair.

"No!" she screamed and fought. Pain seared through her scalp as he yanked her off balance. Demi barely saw the hand as it backslapped her in the face. She went to the ground dazed. Her chest heaved as her head rested in the concrete. The sky above her seemed to be hazy. She could hear her name being yelled. It seemed far off. For a moment, everything went black.

He fought to catch his breath as he held the blonde by the throat to keep her from screaming anymore. He shouldn't have been greedy. He shouldn't have done two.

"Please." He looked at the girl. She had stopped fighting, and what a fight it had been. She merely gripped his wrist.

Her lips moved slightly as all of the breath she had left escaped her. She had a pretty face.

"I'm sorry," he said as he felt her start to weaken. He closed his eyes as he gave a final squeeze. He heard and felt the crack as she went limp.

Demi saw a body fall to the ground. She woke up just as it happened. She knew instantly it was Arizona. She struggled unsuccessfully to her feet and fell against the car. She felt rough hands grab her and through her back in the car.

"You better not try nothin' crazy, or I'll bust your head to the white meat and piss in your skull."

All she could do was cry silently. Despite knowing that a lot of women were kidnapped lately, she foolishly got Arizona to come with her off school property. Sick bastard saw two for the price of one. Maybe Arizona wasn't dead. Maybe he had left her for dead, but she really wasn't. Demi had to get out of the damn car.

The knot was loosening up, and she could feel some relief as blood started to circulate. She would be successful this time. She had to be.

The car stopped moving. Demi leapt forward and flung open the door. He snapped to attention reached back to grab her only catching the tail-end of her skirt. Demi ran. She ran until she couldn't breathe. And he was nowhere to be seen.

He messed up this time. He left one alive and uninjured.

He got too cocky for his own good. Pretty soon, it would be a matter of time before she started talking. She'd seen enough of his face to identify him. He knew he better retreat to his city and lay, low but for whatever reason he couldn't bring himself to do it. He took off around the city to find a new victim, but instead he pulled off into an empty alley and screamed. He was in trouble. He'd messed up, and he thought long and hard before finally going home. Sully's garage was the best place to go. He didn't have much time before Fifty would start looking for the car again.

Get the car detailed and lay low. I have to. It makes no sense not to. Unless, I just wanna get caught. I mean, do I? Have I done this enough? Am I over it? How did it even start? It'll take them a while to find the other girl. Night's coming, and no homeless shithead is going to report it. She was— cold. I had no more use for her. Cold. But her friend, she was warm. I wanted her so bad. She didn't panic. She was quiet. How was I to know the blonde broad was gonna put up a fight? She got me good. A few scratches and a left hook. She fought it off way more than the rest of them did. They must have really wanted to die. The others didn't fight at all. They just died. Sad. They had no will, but those are my favorite kind. It's like doing society a favor; getting rid of the waste. Those girls were nothing needed. They were extra. Superfluous. I did the Earth a favor.

He had lost count of how many favors he had done since last year. It had only been a month since the police started to recognize it. Dumb Fifty. They had been speculating all over the news about who the cab kidnapper was. A white guy in his 40's with deep-rooted psych issues, or someone who lost their will to live so they ran around taking the lives of women because clearly he was a jilted lover. He liked being a mystery. It fascinated him. He had never been a mystery to anyone before. Late 20s, dog and hamster owner, mixed race, loved to play video games and go clubbing. None of this was what they were searching for, and he was okay with that. He would just continue to do what needed to be done.

He closed his eyes and gripped the steering wheel for a moment. He remembered the blonde girl's begging. He remembered how it felt to have her fight back. The feel of his hand around her throat and then… He needed to get to Sully's.

He pulled up to the garage and honked three times. Sully had OCD, but he knew what three honks meant. Once meant regular service. Twice meant coast clear. Three times — well, three times meant help.

"You tapped on that horn like you needa place to hide."

"I do."

"What the fuck did you get yourself into, kid?"

"I don't even think you wanna know. You think I could get a deep clean and a new paint job?"

"I think so. How soon you want her?"

"Now?"

"That's fine. Come back tomorrow — she'll be ready for you."

"I owe you my life."

"Yeah, stop fuckin around, ya weirdo. I'm tired of saving your ass."

"Sully, my dad got you outta plenty of jams before — I think we both know how this works."

"Yeah, yeah, yeah — just make sure this is the last time. I ain't going down for you. I don't care what promises I made your pops ten years ago. And stop being a schmuck and come visit every once in a while!"

"Okay, Sully. You sound just like my dad."

"Well, somebody gotta teach you how ta be a family man. You even seen your ma in the last ten days? You been home? And what about ya sister, huh? You even check up on her? You know that crazy guy is out there, takin' chicks her age!"

"I can assure you — he's not after Violet."

"Only a dummy could be so positive."

"I suppose I'm a fool with a high I.Q."

"Get outta here, kid. I'll see you tomorrow. Don't forget."

"How can I? You got my wheels in your hand."

"Take your other baby out for a spin. She hasn't been opened up in a while." Sully tosses him the keys.

"I'll see you tomorrow, Sully. Be good to my baby."

He drove around the block in the '72 mustang. The engine roared ferociously. He wasn't worried about laying low anymore. As far as he was concerned, he just took care of the problem. The car was getting detailed and repainted, and he was out on the town. He thought about what Sully said about him going home. He hadn't been in a while. In fact, he'd been so consumed with picking up strangers that he skipped going home. Probably couldn't look anyone in their face. Guilt.

Sully was right. I need to go home. I haven't seen them in a couple weeks. I'm sure Mom needs me to do something. I can't just expect Violet to do everything— right? She's only 16. 16, and my mom is damn near dying every day. Yeah. I need to go home. Sometimes the weight of all of this is too much. Too damn much. I can only imagine how Violet feels when I'm not there. I guess I better get my ass there. Yeah. Sully said I should. So, I should.

CHAPTER 2

CALL ME

Miles sat inside of Mr. Foo's restaurant. The place wasn't open yet, but sitting at one of the booths, with the sunlight streaming in, was somehow very peaceful. Her finger brushed her phone screen as she read the news story in front of her. *Damn. This city runs on crime.*

Misty's name popped up on the screen as her phone vibrated. She answered immediately.

"You heard the news?"

"What news?"

"Freakin' deranged taxi driver is putting the city on lockdown. 5 girls victimized all but one dead. Like where the hell has your brain been lately? It's all over the news."

"How was I supposed to know that?"

"Because it's our job to know these things. Misty, what the hell is going on in your head?"

"I'm just a little off today. Sorry."

"We don't do off days. You better fix it. We have girls to save. This whole city is tiptoeing through the damn garden and you're over here forgetting who the hell you are."

"Miles, take it easy. I'm just — I'm having an off day. I'm not gonna blow any cases. I just — something feels off. This shit has me on edge. I mean — what if it was—"

"Zhi? Yea— I keep thinking about that shit. It's boggling my mind. I'm sure some of those girls went to school with Zhi."

"You talk to her about it?"

"Not yet, but I want to."

"You need to. I mean — this shit is huge. It's all over the news. It's crazy."

"I heard you the first time."

"What is your deal?"

"This shit has me on edge. I don't get nervous. I'm not worried for myself, obviously, but I am worried for Zhi. I'm gonna start taking her to school or something until we catch this guy."

Misty didn't say much in response. It had been a couple of weeks since they had solved their last case, which had ended with a very strange and awkward conversation with Miles. The end result being Miles closing her out, and since then, that interaction had not been brought up. All that was going through her head was that Miles might be suspicious of what she was hiding.

Miles' mind was more on Zhi. It wasn't just that this kidnapper was out there picking up girls Zhi's age. Sure, that was an issue. She wanted to take this guy down before something happened to Zhi. Miles almost wanted to take the case on herself and tackle every cab driver in the city. That would take forever. She did know one though she would question. She had seen him around the area before. He had been the one that she had seen drop Daniel off on occasion. No, but Miles was worried about Zhi for another reason. That reason's name was Abby.

"Hello? Earth to Miles—"

"Sorry. What were you saying?"

"I said how much time do you think they'll give it before they call you on the case officially? How many girls do you think will die before finally someone reaches out?"

"I don't know. But I'm not just gonna sit still waiting for them to ask. I'm just gonna reach out. I don't have a boss. I can do what I want. These girls are going missing and we need to help them."

"You're absolutely right."

Miles grabbed the beer off the table she was sitting at and began to really brainstorm. She had no idea where to start, but she needed to act fast. She really didn't want to lose anymore girls. These kids weren't even out of high school. You have to be a sick individual to just think it's okay to torture women —high school girls even more so.

She couldn't wrap her head around it. The more she thought, the more she drank.

Her phone begins to vibrate again.

"Misty, hold on. I gotta take this call." She switches to the incoming call. "Miles here."

"Miles," Captain O'Neal's voice sounded, "you better get your ass to the school right now. There's been another attempt this morning."

"Attempt?"

"Yeah, the girl got away. Her parents are asking for help, and I figured you could meet with them at the school. Who the hell knows where this creep is and if he's looking around to find someone else. I didn't wanna chance it."

"Okay. Hey, did you happen to notice if Zhi got there?"

"Your little neighbor friend? I peeked my head into her class — she's here. No worries."

"I'm on my way."

Miles switched back to Misty on the phone.

"Misty, head down to Zhi's school. Something happened."

"Are we in a hurry?"

"Yes. I want to get down there fast. Meet me there."

She hung up the phone and slid out of the booth. She had been waiting for something, and here it was. She was already dressed and ready for action. The whole way to the school, Miles listened to new stories off of her phone about the kidnappings. She couldn't believe how stupid the media was. They were throwing out facts that weren't even facts.

No wonder this guy was getting away. No one actually knew what they were looking for because the news only wanted to provide a story.

Misty was waiting by her car when Miles pulled up to the school.

"Do they know we're coming?"

"Yes."

"What do you think they're gonna say?"

"What would you say if your kid was almost abducted on her way to school?"

"I don't think there's a right or wrong thing to say about it, actually."

"The wrong thing to say would be 'why weren't they successful?'"

"You have a point."

"This is why I can't have kids."

"Because nobody wants to kidnap them?"

"Because if someone tried, they'd be dead."

"I dunno. Sounds like you've got this parenting thing down."

"If only you knew."

"Are you freaking out? Cause I am in some ways."

"Yeah. Hey you remember that guy that used to drive Daniel around?"

"Umm..."

"You know, the one who was always driving him places when he first got here? Rode around in that big yellow taxi.

Totally knew where everything was, and probably knew everyone too?"

"I mean, what about him?"

"I'm thinking maybe he can get us a map to whatever or wherever we need to know. Most cab drivers have a map that's off-grid for most of us regular people. If he has one, we can cover a lot more ground. I'm thinking about seeing if I can locate him."

"Hmm."

"What do you think?"

"I mean, it could work. I dunno. Do you even know where to find him?"

"I don't need to know. I have you for that kinda thing."

"Yeah, but I haven't seen him since Daniel was arrested."

"Okay, but you've never had any issues getting in touch with anyone before. So, do what I ask."

"I just don't see the point like what if he has no answers?"

"You're acting weird as hell right now. Like you don't know the proper protocol. If he doesn't have answers it's simple; we let his ass go. Like we let everyone else go. What in the world are you talking about right now?"

"I'm just…"

"Snap out of it and do your job."

"Excuse me?"

"I don't know what you have going on, but I need you here. Focused on the situation. So whatever it is, please snap out of it and do your job."

Miles never had to get on Misty before, but clearly it was necessary this time. Misty never offered up such excuses before, and it was plain weird. Why was she so defensive over a cab driver she didn't even know? Even more so, why did it matter what happened if he knew or didn't know certain things? Any other time she would have just complied. Miles didn't want to get into it with her. After so many years of working as a team it was bound to happen; the clashing of two alphas. Miles grew irritated with her rather quickly. Of course, over the past couple of weeks, she had lost patience with Misty soon and sooner. Something was happening to their relationship, and Miles couldn't stop it. She couldn't think about that at the moment though.

They were brought into the school office. Miles immediately saw the situation for what it was. Demetria Slochim sat there with her parents. Her gaze was lost as everyone talked around her. She hugged her arms on lap. Her hair was a stringy mess. Tear stains had left their marks on her cheeks. She was not okay. She had gotten away. Her friend had not. Miles could see the guilt on the girl's face and knew the very real feeling of the scene playing over and over again in the girl's mind.

CHAPTER 3

"Miles, this is Mr. and Mrs. Slochim and their daughter Demetria. She was one of the young ladies fortunate enough to get away from this guy."

Miles blocked the parents view of their daughter. She wanted the girl to focus. Also, parents didn't tend to like her method of questioning.

"Demetria, is that what you like to be called?"

"Demi," the girl choked out. She coughed as if she had been silent this whole time while the adults talked.

"Demi, then," Miles said. "I'm Miles, and I'm going to catch the guy that did this to you. Can you tell me what happened?"

Demi swallowed hard as she collected her thoughts. She didn't meet Miles' eyes with her own, though. They stayed glued to anything that wasn't human in the room.

"Arizona and I decided to go out for lunch, and we thought it would be fun to do a longer lunch that usual. The period after lunch is boring, so we didn't think we would miss much. She wanted to take the bus back, but I thought the cab would be safe. She was always worrying about something, and I knew that there were kidnappings going on, but what were the odds it would happen to us? We got in the cab, and she was the one who noticed that we were going the wrong direction. We were going to jump out at a stop light and run, but he turned into an alley and dragged me out of the car." Tears began to flow freely as the girl shook. "Arizona tried to stop him, but he hit me really hard and I blacked out for a bit while he took her away."

Miles sat forward.

"What happened after that? How did you get away, Demi?"

"I-I," she tried to control her sobs, "I woke up in the back seat of the car. My hands were tied. I got them free and jumped out of the car when it slowed down. I ran to the closest diner and stayed in a booth until my parents arrived."

"What do you remember about the car, Demi?"

"It—it was a cab."

"No, other than that. Sights, smells, sounds: anything else? What about the alley where he knocked you out?"

Miles felt a hand on her shoulder, and she spun around quickly, grabbing the hand. Demi's father was furious.

"My daughter is hurt and suffering. She needs rest."

"Your daughter needs to focus," Miles said. "Or would you rather him come back for her because she's the only job he didn't finish?"

He looked like he was about to slap her, and Miles glared him, daring him to try. Demi grabbed Miles' arm.

"I could pick out his eyes in a lineup. They were soulless. He had no real feelings. He just— was. He was cold. And he took my best friend from me— There's no doubt in my mind that Arizona is dead. He had to have killed her, and if she wasn't dead when he left her — she's dead by now. She wouldn't be able to survive this kind of trauma. She was born with an extremely bad heart and this kinda thing would have sent her straight into cardiac arrest. She had her inhaler but that wouldn't stop her heart from beating out of her chest. I tried to keep her calm, I really did. I tried to tell her that everything would be okay, but she knew something about the cabbie didn't feel right. She was smarter than me. I wish— like hell— I would have listened to her."

"Do you remember where you guys were when he—"

"I would remember it again if I saw it. The boroughs are huge though. We'd have to literally go everywhere before I saw it again. But I'd know. I just can't think off the top of my head. It was about 10 minutes away from the alley I escaped into. I know that much because I looked at the clock. I dunno if that helps or not."

"It helps a lot more than you know. I promise you —

we're gonna get this guy. And when we do, I'm gonna make sure he goes away for a very long time."

"For Arizona?"

"For Arizona."

Miles never made promises she couldn't keep. She was determined to make sure she caught this guy. There was a little girl out there Zhi's age that got killed — that went to Zhi's school, might have ate lunch with her, might have had classes with her — and this is way too close for comfort. There were too many buttons that this pushed. She looked at Misty, who seemed zoned out. Maybe she was thinking about her mother. Miles didn't know all the details, because no one knew them. When Misty was a little girl, her mother had disappeared, never to be heard from again. No one knew what happened to her. Now, there was a guy out there picking up girls like groceries and discarding them like trash.

"Is there anything you need from us?"

Mr. Slochim seemed to soften a little. Miles understood that he was concerned. He allowed his daughter to speak freely even though some things were painful to hear. It was a tough thing to push through. Something happened to his family that was out of his control. Miles matched his demeanor.

"I'm not worried about my fee just yet. I dunno what you do for a living, but this is what I do, and I promise I'll do it. It may take a little while, but I'll get it done. You can count on that."

"I don't care what it costs. Money is no object. Whatever resources you may need, I can assure you I can afford to provide them for you."

Miles noticed that Mrs. Slochim hadn't said much. She didn't even wince at the sordid details of her child's attempted kidnapping. In fact, she sat there stone cold the entire time.

"I appreciate that. I just hope that we can solve this expediently for Arizona's memory. Your daughter is in good hands. If I need to send a few guys over your way so that you are protected…"

"I assure you, that is already in place. My daughter is my world, and to think someone, some monster was trying to take her from us makes me angry. I'm no detective, but I think my girl was just in the wrong place at the wrong time. There didn't seem to be any premeditation. I'm more than positive this person is just picking at random, because if he had any kind of clue of who Demetria is and who her family is, he wouldn't have touched her. He has no idea who he messed with."

Miles chewed on her lip a little.

"And just who is that, Mr. Slochim?"

The man closed his mouth. He realized that he had said too much. Captain O'Neal cleared his throat.

"Well, I think we've got what we needed. We will be in touch with your family as soon as we find anything."

"Thank you," Mr. Slochim nodded. His wife and daughter both stood up. As he passed Miles, he stuck out a business card. She took it. "We will talk, detective. Sometime and somewhere better. I will explain some things to you."

"I look forward to it," Miles said curiously. Miles cleared up a few things with the captain before she walked out of the school where Misty had escaped to after the Slochims had left.

"What is your deal?"

"What?"

"You're too quiet."

"Am I?"

"Cut the shit, will you? What is going on in that head of yours?"

"Too much."

"Well, I have time, so—"

"And I don't."

"Huh?"

"I'm just — look, I don't wanna get into this right now. I don't even know what's happening, but I have the strangest feeling that this might be closer to home than we think, and that's really fuckin' unsettling for me. Seriously."

"And you think this whole thing isn't unsettling for me? I mean, I know what you've gone through. I get it. It's not cool, but you know exactly why this case is important to me. I have people important in my life, too. So let's not pretend you're the only one feeling unsettled about this."

"I'm sorry. I didn't — you know that feeling you get

when something just isn't right, but you're afraid to look deeper into it?"

"I don't think I'm following."

"I just have a really bad feeling about all of this. And it's freaking me out. And I'm sorry that I'm acting like this, but dammit — seeing that girl, knowing she was almost taken — really messed with me. I wanna catch this guy. I really do."

"So then let's fuckin' catch him. No excuses."

"Okay."

"Great. We've been a team for too long to be second-guessing each other. So let's make this count. Okay?"

"Are you second-guessing me?"

"What are you talking about?"

Misty closed her eyes.

"Miles, I'm not the only one who has been acting weird. And if it's about the kiss you saw between me and Diego, then you should know that there was nothing there. Literally nothing, and even if there was, it isn't your problem."

Miles pursed her lips together.

"I'm fine. It was just… the case at that time — and I was thinking about a lot." *A lot meaning lying to Zhi, fantasizing about Misty, sleeping with Abby, and Shoni's disappearance. 'A lot' was an understatement.*

Miles could tell that Misty was deciding on whether or not she believed her friend, but whether she did or not, Misty wasn't going to spill anything on her end. Miles didn't push, but she knew something was up. Something was bothering her, and she needed answers. Her best friend was already dreading figuring out who this monster was, but why was she acting like this? Miles wasn't going to push though. Why push when she wasn't going to confess what her own demons were.

Suddenly, Misty changed her demeanor.

"I know what we need."

"What?" Miles asked with a frown. Misty shook her head.

"Leave it to me. In the meantime, I'm going to see what can be done about the cab company. There's gotta be something the cops have missed."

"There's always something the cops have missed," Miles quipped. Misty laughed.

"Whatever. I'll let you know what I find," she said, and began to walk back to her car.

CHAPTER 4

I must be outta my damn mind! All signs point to something I don't even wanna address. I don't wanna deal with this. I don't wanna feel all these feelings. I most definitely don't want my best friend to start questioning my integrity because I'm choosing to keep quiet. I know that I'm off. I know that you can read me like a book but dammit — I don't know what else there is to do. How do I— I don't want to— Ugh. Never mind. But I can't just ignore it. I mean, if it is what I'm thinking — and if Zhi were to get hurt — how would I even begin to explain myself to Miles? There is no explanation, honestly. How do I say I might know exactly who this man is? All of the signs are pointing in the same direction. I just wish they weren't and I'd rather know before just putting it out there. Either way — Miles is gonna wanna kill me. Guilt by association. Fuck. Why am I having such a hard time with this? I

mean, we just met — kind of. For whatever reason, I can't bring myself to say anything about this guy, because if it is who I think it is — I'm fucked. I'm just fucked. I know I am.

Seeing Demi at the school really shook Misty up. This was real. That girl could be dead if she hadn't gotten away, and — she needed answers.

She sent the text, and then drove over to the hotdog shack that he usually frequented on his shifts. She wasn't a fan of hotdogs. Maybe it was the name, but they were a weird and awkward food that made her think like she was eating part of an animal.

Just as she thought, he was there. His smile beamed like morning sunlight when she approached, but today, it didn't faze her. She pulled up a chair close to him.

"Yo! Where you been?"

"I could ask you the same question."

"What you talking about, baby?"

"No — don't even."

"What's wrong?"

"I haven't heard from you in 8 days, Boston. 8 whole days. There's a maniac hacking up little girls, and you're nowhere to be found. Boston — where the hell have you been?"

"I've been working!"

"Yeah — and that means don't pick up your phone and call to check on anyone?"

"That means I don't have time to argue with you about any of this foolishness. I'm grown. I don't have to answer to you when it comes to my whereabouts. That's not what this is nor has it ever been."

"Oh — so you think you're not supposed to tell me you're okay?"

"I think you're overreacting."

"I'm less than underwhelmed with the way you're behaving right now. I love you and I love spending time with you, but dammit, you better get your shit together. How do I know…"

"How do you know *what*? That it's not me? Go ahead and say it. That's what you're thinking isn't it? That it's been me all along? You couldn't wait to just bring it this way huh? You knew damn well I was gonna be busy this week. Especially with all the festivals downtown. I told you in advance — so you don't get to act upset, dammit!"

"You think that I think it's you? What kinda monster would you be if I thought that? Or me for that matter? What kinda monster would I be to just stick it through with you after knowing that shit? I'll tell you in case you wanna know — I wouldn't be shit. You know this right? Don't ever try to reduce me just because. Not cool. If I thought for a second it was you — we wouldn't be talking."

But she did think it was him. And judging by his response, he knew it too. He knew it when she asked where he'd been, when she flipped out, when she tried to recover from accusations; he knew what she thought of him, and that was a hard pill to swallow.

"And why are we talking now?"

"You tell me. Because clearly I only think the worst of you. Clearly I'm accusing you of being a horrible person. I don't know any horrible people just to let you know."

"We all know horrible people. We just don't like to admit it."

"What does that mean?"

"That no one is who we think they are. We all have secrets we carry with us daily. Some of us are just better at keeping them in the dark. Can you honestly say that I know everything about you? There's nothing you might have left out? Things you're saving for later? Or not at all? 'Cause if you can honestly say that, you might just be a miracle. Nobody in the free world is *that* honest. Nobody. And if they say they are, they're lying. Basically."

"So when do you lie to me?"

"I don't."

"That makes no sense."

"I don't have to lie to you — yet. There will come a time when I will lie to you. I haven't yet. I haven't had a reason to. Everyone lies, babe. Everyone. And one day I'm gonna lie to you, and we're most likely gonna fight about it, and when it happens I'm gonna remind you of this day when I said eventually I'm gonna lie to you. It might be something super small or ginormous but either way a lie is a lie. Right?"

"Right."

"Have you ever lied to me?"

"I haven't felt the need to."

"Okay then. And one of these days you will feel the need to. And you know what's gonna happen? I'm gonna be okay with it because I know I'm not perfect and I've been in that situation before where I felt like a lie was better than the truth. People can act like they tell the truth no matter what but we know better. We know different. It's impossible to always tell the truth. Sometimes your mind your heart just won't let you — especially if it may be harmful. I don't like to hurt people. So sometimes a white lie is easier. If that makes you upset, I understand, but sometimes I find it easier than telling the absolute truth. I've seen the truth break people. I don't intend on breaking anyone."

"The crazy thing is, while it makes sense to you, I've seen a lie break up happy homes. So, we can't both be right, can we?"

"I don't think we can."

She didn't trust him anymore. He basically just confirmed that he had no problem with lying to her in order to protect her feelings. How did he expect her to digest that information? What was she supposed to do? Just sit there and take it? It wasn't going to happen that way, and he knew it. He wanted her to just roll over and take it, but it wasn't even that type of party. He confirmed her suspicions enough to warrant her to be careful. Who knew what secrets he was already hiding? What kind of dumbass admits they're a liar? She put on a reassuring face.

"Okay. I get it. I'm gonna need something from you,

though. If you can't do it, it's fine, but if you can, that'd be great, too. I dunno if it's true or not, so I figured I would ask you if you ever heard of an off-grid map for the city?"

"I'm a taxi driver. Of course I have."

"Do you think you could get me one? I just wanna see it. I heard about it and it sounded pretty cool; so, I'd love to see one. If it's just a taxi driver thing then I get it, but it would mean a lot to me if you could."

"I mean, I guess I could as long as you promise not to tell anyone you have it. I could get into a lot of shit giving you my map."

"I promise."

Boston looked into her eyes. She was genuine. He could tell. From the moment he met Misty, he knew that she was good. Deep down, she was nothing but good. He wasn't sure what they were. They had started spending every night together just talking then kissing then they both realized that they liked each other. She was special. He didn't want to screw this up. Grabbing her hand and squeezing it, he nodded towards the door.

"I got one in the cab. C'mon, let's go get it."

Misty nodded. She wasn't sure how she was going to play, but she didn't want to go to Miles with this. *This* she wanted to take care of herself.

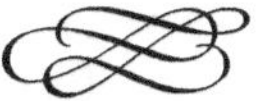

CHAPTER 5

LAY LOW

He hadn't been home in a while. So, it was quite the surprise when he walked through the door and saw his mother cooking in the kitchen.

"Bubby? Is that you?"

"Yeah ma, it's me."

"Your sister, she said something happened at school. Some bad man took her friends away? Do you know anything about this? Is it safe out there?"

"I don't know anything about it, Ma. If it's someone in my circle, he has hell to pay. Everyone knows not to go near my sister, Ma. Everyone. I won't stand for it."

He started to feel uneasy. Lying to his mom was not something he was ever able to get away with as a kid. It was one of the reasons that he tried avoiding her. Lying to her was necessary. He had to protect himself, but also her. Her heart was weak. What could he say? Yes, I know about it because it's me? Yes, I hurt those girls? Yes, it was me, Ma? He had to lie. Besides, if she knew her little boy was capable of doing what he had been doing, she would never forgive him. She would die of a broken heart.

As far as Violet was concerned, he wasn't going to hurt her. He would die before letting anything hurt her, including his own demons. It didn't matter how bad his urges got, and they were bad, he wouldn't hurt her. He used to be able to ignore them; he would just fantasize. That went away quickly. Soon, he had to have a fix.

He looked up quickly. His mother was talking.

"Bubby? You never were any good at lying."

"Ma, I don't know anything. Nothing at all. I just know that this has everyone in the neighborhood running scared all of a sudden, and I don't like it. I also know sometimes the media hypes things up way worse than they are."

"Bubby, you listen to me, and you listen to me good. I am not about to be responsible for anything. If you know who did it, you better turn them in. They'll come you know — come looking for you because the people you're protecting won't protect you. You and I both know it's true. You're looking for someone to save you and have your back, but really, there's no loyalty amongst crooks. Turn them in if you know something, or next thing you know, it'll be your face on the news for something you didn't do."

"Ma, I promise you, I don't know anything. If I did, I would have said something already. I just really don't like the idea that there's a guy out there snatching girls like that.

"Keep your eyes open. Those people around you are always on the move. You better move with them. I don't mean move in the same direction. I mean move out of their way. Watch them like a hawk. They'll slip up soon."

The old woman held a warning in her tone. He didn't even know what to say. She always believed him no matter what. He didn't know what he would do if she found out. He wasn't ready to send his mother into an early grave. But being honest was out of the question. This was one of those secrets he would have to take to the grave. He didn't mind it so much, but carrying such a heavy secret was lonely.

Am I wrong? Of course I am. I lied to my mother. To her face — and I don't even feel bad. I just feel like it was necessary. I know I let my mom down. I let my whole family down. I even let myself down and I can't even blame it on a disease. This all just got outta hand too quickly. I mean — one minute it was one girl, then it was four, and the fifth got away. It's only a matter of time before I get caught. It's only a matter of time before the guilt eats away at me — but I must confess, it feels good getting away with murder. Literally and figuratively. Just sitting here has my heart jumping out of my chest. I can feel it thumping harshly. I wish there was something I could do. I have no right to feel bad for myself though. I brought this all on myself. I've been lying. I've been sneaking around and hurting women and I deserve whatever it is I get. My mom knows something is up. She has no idea how involved I am, though. I don't think she could even attempt to understand how deep I'm into this. Damn. You really blew it this time. It wasn't enough just messing with the girls — you made them disappear. Violet — she's just so naïve — this literally could happen to her, if the killer wasn't me. You're disgusting, dude. How could you just do that? Like — I don't understand what you thought this would be. I still hear that girl screaming. I've never heard anything like that before. She was so scared. So frightened. I just wanted her to shut up. I needed her to and the only way to do that was to literally make her disappear. Her friend, she was scared, but in a different way. I can remember the look of terror on her face when I turned down that last alleyway. She had no idea where her friend was — no understanding whatsoever — and the craziest part? She was smart enough to get away. I didn't want to admit this, but part of me let her get away so she could — or I could get caught. Do you have any idea how miserable this is for me? Living like this. I'd love to blame it on something. I wish I knew which part of my brain was broken, honestly. I wish I knew which part they could cut out so I could be normal. If they could cut out part of my brain — the part that misbehaves and kills women — I would have that surgery yesterday. I've never hurt a soul — but now that's all I do. I can't even say it makes me feel powerful because it doesn't, it makes me feel... empty once it's all said and done. Empty as fuck. That last girl, she — I think she died before I even got rid of her. She was freaking out pretty heavy, too. I didn't even know what to do. She wouldn't shut up. She just kept screaming and acting crazy. I hated it. I was anxious the whole time. I keep going back to that part. I can't escape it. She's not who I thought she was — she's my one. The one I'll remember no matter what. She's going to haunt me forever.

"Ma, do you think Jesus forgives everyone, even the ones that break the commandments?"

"Why? Do you need to be forgiven for something?"

"Ma, don't reach like that."

"What do you mean? If there's something you need, we can go to church and get Father Mauricio to pray for you and then you'll do some Hail Marys and be done with it. Don't make this more difficult than it has to be. I don't like it. You asking me questions is leading me to thinking that you have something on your mind. What is it? What did you do? Or what do you think you might have done to need forgiveness from Jesus?"

"It was a rhetorical question. I haven't done anything, but I still have to question it. I've been reading my word more, and I had to say something. I have questions and just want some answers. That's all, Ma."

Easy does it, jackass. Don't give her any reason to keep going. You've never been good at lying to her. Never. She already suspects you. Dammit. You always figure out a way to get her on your ass. Always. You can never just slide through without her being suspicious. She knows you. Really knows you — and Violet, she knows you too.

"Where's Violet?"

"She'll be coming through the door soon. I'm surprised you didn't go pick her up with all the craziness happening. Why wouldn't you?"

"I — Violet can take of herself. I know for a fact. Like I said, they wouldn't dare touch her. If it's anyone who knows me. It's not happening. They know me, and they know better."

"You been doing stuff you have no business doing in those streets again, haven't you? How many bodies? How many times you think I'm gonna wash all the blood out of your clothes and not question nothing? How many people you knocked off? You think I don't know what you do? I know. I see! You come in here riddled with guilt and confusion and I don't say nothing. I just keep doing what I'm supposed to do. I protect you."

"You think I don't protect you? I don't see no dad around here! I been him and me for the longest. Or did you forget? I protect Violet, too. You don't remember who makes sure she's got everything she needs? Oh. I forgot. It couldn't possibly be me. It's that man in the sky, right? Not the sacrifices I make."

"If your father were here, you wouldn't be talking to me like this."

"No…"

"You only talk to me like this because you know that he's not here, but if he was, he would beat you. He wouldn't even allow you to look at me with that judgment in your eyes. You think 'cause I got sick you can just come here and talk to me anyway you want to. My boy, my baby, had more respect for me before I was sick. You probably don't even remember it. It's been so long since I was normal."

"Ma, you are normal. And I'm sorry. I didn't mean to disrespect you. I just — all this talk about this guy — it's got me on edge. You just don't know how bad it is sometimes. I literally think about this shit hoping I don't get a phone call. Hoping it will be over soon so I can know that Violet is safe, but it just keeps going. That guy is a damn psycho and what do we have? Nothing. Not a damn thing. We don't know anything. Not a description of this guy, not an ounce of a clue. How am I to know it's not one of those damn teachers that moonlight as a driver? Or even the principal for that matter? We just don't know and that kills me. How could we not know anything?"

"Romans 1, 18 through 20."

"Huh?"

"For the wrath of God is revealed from heaven against all ungodliness and unrighteousness of men, who by their unrighteousness suppress the truth. For what can be known about God is plain to them, because God has shown it to them. For his invisible attributes, namely, his eternal power and divine nature, have been clearly perceived, ever since the creation of the world, in the things that have been made. So, they are without excuse."

"Why do you always do that?"

"I raised you to know your word."

"You also raised me to question things, but when I question things like this you get upset."

"Proverbs 3, 1 through 35."

"My son, do not forget my teaching, but let your heart keep my commandments, for length of days and years of life and peace they will add to you. Let not steadfast love and faithfulness forsake you; bind them around your neck; write them on the tablet of your heart. So, you will find favor and good success in the sight of God and man. Trust in the Lord with all your heart, and do not lean on your own understanding. Yeah, I know, I know — but what does it mean? Sometimes I don't think I get the message."

"Or maybe you do, and you just don't want to. Revelation 22, 1 through 21."

"Then the angel showed me the river of the water of life, bright as crystal, flowing from the throne of God and of the Lamb through the middle of the street of the city; also, on either side of the river, the tree of life with its twelve kinds of fruit, yielding its fruit each month. The leaves of the tree were for the healing of the nations. No longer will there be anything accursed, but the throne of God and of the Lamb will be in it, and his servants will worship him. They will see his face, and his name will be on their foreheads. And night will be no more. They will need no light of lamp or sun, for the Lord God will be their light, and they will reign forever and ever."

"Yes, you know your word, too. I instilled it in you."

"Ma, I know it, but I don't necessarily believe in it anymore."

"Yes, you do."

The front door opened. Violet's eyes were red from crying, but her current facial expression was more of confusion and disgust. He knew it was for him.

"What are you doing here?"

"I still live here, last time I checked."

"Does it count as living here if you are never here?"

"I'm here today."

Violet huffed.

"Like it matters." She placed her backpack on the floor. She loved her brother, but she didn't feel like showing it now. He left. He always left, but this time he left when she needed him. That might have been forgivable, but since he didn't come back…

"Are you okay?"

"Wow! It's been weeks, and you're just now asking me if I'm okay? Why? Because you wanna feel like a big man? Feel like the hero? Where the hell have you been! You didn't even call. I was walking through the boroughs by myself. By myself! There was a man out there killing girls! My age! Four girls from my school. Two of them in my class. And you wanna ask me if I'm okay? No! I'm not, and I don't think I ever will be. But thanks. Thanks so much for pretending to care."

He didn't even know how to respond. She was right. She checked him. She let him know exactly how she felt. He was shitty. A shitty brother. And asking her if she was alright after two weeks of not even bothering to call was not the brightest thing to do. He meant well— but it was stupid. How could he ask a question he already knew the answer to?

"I didn't mean to…"

"To just leave us here while there was a crazy man out there? Yeah, we know."

"Come on Vi, I just — I was trying to make sure you guys were gonna be okay. I secured my spot. I secured your safety."

Violet rolled her eyes. He didn't get it. No matter how she explained it. No matter how passionately she spoke, it all came down to him being the hero. Him being the savior. He didn't understand that nothing replaced him actually being there. Nothing. Their mother sat in disbelief of all the things she heard from the two of them. These couldn't be her children. Never. Her children didn't talk like that. Her voice shook as she spoke.

"John 15, verses 12 through 17."

Violet looked at her brother and sighed.

"This is my commandment, that you love one another as I have loved you. Greater love has no one than this, that someone lay down his life for his friends. You are my friends if you do what I command you. No longer do I call you servants, for the servant does not know what his master is doing; but I have called you friends, for all that I have heard from my Father I have made known to you. You did not choose me, but I chose you and appointed you that you should go and bear fruit and that your fruit should abide, so that whatever you ask the Father in my name, he may give it to you."

"So you know what that means, right?"

"That we need to abide," her son said. They got tired of quoting scriptures. The Bible was real to her but it was no longer real to them. Not after they lost their father, but of course they still knew their word. They could recite some verses backwards and forwards without even so much of a thought. And they knew it. When Mama asked — you'd better oblige. Even if they didn't believe, they still respected her beliefs.

"You are my children and I love you. I have made sacrifices but ultimately, I have brought you to know and love God. Whether you agree right now or not. I need you both— to get yourselves together. I know you love each other. I know this whole thing has you both on edge. So, I'm asking that you find more reasons to be on one accord than you do to be at each other's throats. Please. I don't ask for much. Just this."

Violet looked down.

"It bothers me that you weren't here when I needed you. It bothers me that my brother has a cab, and he didn't think to drive my way — to make sure I made it home and to school okay. It bothers me you didn't call to even see if this affected me. Because it does, you know? It affects me. Super bad."

"I'm sorry sis. I really am. I didn't mean to…"

"To run like you always do? We're a family of runners. I just thought…"

"Thought this situation should have been handled differently."

"Yes."

"You're actually right. I love you. And I wouldn't deliberately hurt you, you know that."

"I know."

She did know. It still hurt, and it still hit close to home knowing that her brother was running from something that he couldn't share. In fact, it did more than hurt. It scared her.

Violet grabbed her bag and went to her room. She wasn't mad anymore but having that conversation in front of their mom was intense. She hated when her mom made them quote the Bible. It wasn't necessarily that she didn't believe in it — but she was skeptical in her own right.

Her brother was never the type to let things stew for too long. He felt like all problems should be handled accordingly and head on. There was no need for time in between. He couldn't let it go. Guilt. He was prideful like his father. He always had to be right or make things right. The genes were single handedly handed down from his great grands to him. He hated it but he couldn't fight it. He knocked on her door and let himself in. He never waited for her to say come in— he knew he'd be waiting forever. She never invited him in. She was a teenage girl after all.

He knocked on her bedroom door. There was a muffled response, and he walked in. She sat on her bed looking at her phone.

"Vi, I…"

"Why did it take you so long to come back?"

He shook his head.

He really did mess up. When their father was away in Iraq… he didn't come back. They waited and waited, but he never came back. They held out hope and prayed to every God they could think of — but he was gone. That was a definitive moment for them. The moment they learned to stop praying. The moment they no longer believed in prayer.

"I'm sorry, Vi." He hugged her and all they could do was tear up.

"Do you know the guy that's doing this?"

"No."

"Are you sure?"

"I may have a feeling. But I don't want you to be worried either way. I can take you to school and pick you up until they catch the guy."

"Or you can finally fix up dad's car for me."

"Or I could do that."

"So, do that."

"You're so damn bossy sometimes."

"I wouldn't be myself if I wasn't."

"So, I can get the car fixed in a couple days. But until then I'm driving you everywhere. Deal?"

"Everywhere?"

He looked at her like he might kill her.

"If you keep going, I promise you…"

"Okay! Okay! Everywhere. Sheesh."

"Yeah, so tell your boyfriend you can't hook up with him after school for a while. I'm sure he'll understand." A painful expression showed on Violet's face. He saw her choke back a cry. "Vi, what's wrong?"

"I don't have a boyfriend."

"Oh, great…"

"But — I had a girlfriend."

"Had?"

"Her name was Arizona." She showed him her phone screen, and he felt his stomach churn and twist into knots as he saw the familiar face. "She's one of the missing girls; the one missing from today."

Fuck. I didn't — yes, I did.

He closed his eyes. He could hear her cries. He could feel her struggle. He could see her wide eyes begging him. He felt the snap of her neck.

"Are you sure she was one of the ones on the news?"

"Yeah, very sure. And, please don't tell Mom. Only a few people knew we were — we were in love. Like really in love. Like 'Oh my God!' amazing love. Like I couldn't wait to see her in the morning love. Like I woulda married her after college kinda love. Now, they're saying that, that she might be — you don't think she's dead, do you?"

He reached out and hugged her again to avoid looking in her eyes.

"I didn't even know you liked girls."

"We all have secrets."

Yes. Yes, we do.

CHAPTER 6

THE LOCKET

iles sat in her car outside the neon sign. She didn't want to go in. Something about the place made her feel like she was outing herself, even though there were plenty of men who walked in and stumbled out with exhausted grins on their damn faces. She wanted to look every one of them up and call their wives, because they definitely had them. Wives, fiancées, girlfriends - all these guys were just trying to get a fix. A small voice in side of Miles asked if she wasn't trying to do the same thing. Sure, she wasn't in a relationship per se, but she was trying to escape it.

It was late when the door opened, and Abby walked out of the building, looking like she had a hard day. Miles didn't get out of the car right away. She really wasn't sure what she was going to say to Abby. They had mostly texted

49

in the past few weeks. Tonight, she felt like seeing her —
seeing someone. She glanced at her phone. Misty hadn't
returned her text from an hour ago. That meant she was
busy — too busy for her.

"Abby!" Miles called out. Abby turned and waved as
Miles jogged up to her.

"Hey, you. Were you waiting for me?"

"Um… yeah. That's weird, right?"

Abby shrugged.

"I've never had anyone wait on me — well, wait outside
at least." She smiled and bounced on her feet. "So, is this a
social call or…"

"No! I mean, no," Miles laughed nervously. "You're
probably tired from work, and…"

"And I could use a drink," Abby said. "And company
that's pretty damn sexy."

"I knew I was just arm candy to you," Miles smirked.
"You had me at drink though."

They walked to a bar around the corner. Miles wasn't
used to drinking out. Her stash in the fridge was enough to
last a doomsday prophecy coming true.

"I can't believe this shit is going on," Abby slammed her
beer down. "I hate that a girl can't even feel safe in broad
daylight."

"That's why I'm going to catch the bastard and make
him wish he was never born," Miles said. Abby rested her
hand on Miles'.

"I know you will, babe. You've got this."

"There's just no rhyme or reason for why he's killing these girls. If I knew that, then I could connect something."

"Maybe you should stop looking for this motive to be rational."

Miles frowned.

"What do you mean?"

Abby crossed her legs on the bar stool.

"Listen, I've learned that if there isn't a reason, then that is the reason. What if this guy is battling the desire to kill these girls? What if he's mentally battling some sort of demon? He could just be losing the battle, and in that moment, he snaps. He takes the next girl that comes around and — well, you know."

Miles didn't want her to be right. If she was right, then that meant, she was looking for someone who didn't even know fully what was going on.

"So, how's Misty?"

Miles looked up quickly.

"Huh?"

"How's Misty? You've neglected to mention her in any of our conversations lately." She rubbed her finger around the rim of her beer. "You've mentioned the old man and his grandkids, but not her."

"It's kind of weird to be sleeping with you and talking about another girl."

"No judgement," Abby raised her hands. "I told you that there were no strings attached."

"Well, we're kind of on the outs at the moment. I mean,

we're still working together, but… she's hiding something from me. Something I can't figure out."

"Maybe she's gay." Miles frowned at Abby's chuckle. "Sorry. I just — when two people in a relationship hide something from each other, then the other person can sense it. They start to hide their true feelings. Misty, on some level knows you're not being your true self with her."

"I feel like you're just trying to get me to come out to her."

"And you're trying to act like you aren't afraid that Misty might actually want to give this whole thing a try."

Miles shook her head. She both loved and hated Abby. The door opened to the bar, and clear shouting could be heard from the streets outside. Miles caught the glimpse of several individuals running by the bar. One of them looked familiar.

"Hold on, Abby." She slid off her seat and start running out of the bar. A girl lay on the ground next to a sedan yelling and screaming as she covered up her face. A group of guys and girls were in the middle of a brawl. One guy threw another guy against a store front next to the bar while a girl jumped on his back and began to scratch at his face.

"Miles?" Abby's voice appeared from behind her.

Miles didn't answer. Instead she charged up to the guy with the girl on his back. Yanking the girl off and throwing her onto the ground, Miles placed a foot on the girl's chest before she could get up. The guy turned around.

"Miles?"

"Chao!" Miles growled. "What the fuck!"

"Hey, get off of her!" a guy started to grab Miles. She sent a fist into his nose and slammed her foot into his knee cap. She reached into her back pocket and pulled out the small gun that she carried.

"Hey!" She yelled. "Get outta here!"

Choruses of voices announcing the presence of a gun. Caused the entire group to abandon the fight and start to scatter.

"Not you!" Miles yelled at Chao. He raised his hands up.

"Not moving."

Miles looked back at Abby who had a perplexed, and yet, amused look on her face.

"Sorry," Miles grimaced. "Abby, this is Chao aka the idiot."

"Nice to meet you." Abby pointed to him. "You've got some blood on your face."

Chao touched his cheek and winced. Miles punched him in the arm.

"Come on. We're leaving."

"Forget you, Miles." Chao stormed off. Miles sighed as she turned to Abby again.

"Go ahead," Abby said before Miles could say anything. "Go take care of him. We'll talk soon."

Miles nodded and ran to get her car. Chao hadn't made it very far when she pulled up beside him.

"Hey, get in." Chao ignored her. "I'm going to keep

doing this until we get home, and you know how annoying I can be. You might as well get in."

Chao stopped walking and stood for a moment with his head leaning back staring into the sky. Finally, he walked around the side of the car and got in.

"Why are you doing this?"

"Because from what I saw back there, you're clearly out of your mind running with that crew."

"You don't even know what that crew is, Miles."

"Then tell me, Chao."

"Nah, I'm good. You don't need to know, and I don't need you sticking your nose in where it doesn't belong."

They rode in silence for a while. She felt bad. Even though Chao was only a little younger than her, she had always considered him a younger brother and friend. He didn't need that. He needed someone good in his life, and she was barely able to be anything for Zhi. Of course, it was easier to pay more attention to Zhi. She was a girl, and she already looked up to Miles. Chao didn't look up to anyone — at least, not that she knew of.

"It's still kind of early. You want to hang out for a bit?" Chao's expression mimicked the shock that she felt as well. She wasn't sure where the request came from, but it was genuine.

"Miles, I don't need you babysitting me."

"Trust me, I'm not. I'm not even sure why I'm offering this, but we used to be closer. Fuck it. Let's go to Charlie's. I bet he still has that skee-ball machine that we used to play on. If I win, you buy the food. If you win, I buy."

She half-expected Chao to tell her to fuck off, but he shrugged and nodded.

Charlie's was one of those 24/7 cafés that attracted more patrons at night than during the day. It wasn't for the great food. The food was actually pretty average. Everybody just loved Charlie. Miles felt bad that she hadn't been to the place in years. Charlie didn't give her any grief about that when they walked into the cafe, either.

"What? You two are bored, so you decide to come in. You expect me to serve you food?"

"You can't be mad at us, Charlie," Miles said. "You know we've always been your favorite people."

"Fine. I won't admit it, but I will get you food."

"Actually," Chao said. "We need something else first. You have that skee-ball machine still?"

It was almost one in the morning when the two of them got back to Foo's. They were both laughing.

"It was good to hang out, Miles. Thanks."

"Whatever," Miles said. "Just remember who won tonight. Skee-ball champ."

"I let you win," Chao said. "Just like I always did."

The door opened to Foo's apartment, and Zhi stuck her head out. She frowned when she saw Miles.

"Zhi," Miles said. Suddenly, she remembered everything that happened today. She really hadn't checked in on Zhi.

Zhi ignored Miles and looked at Chao.

"Did you get it?"

Chao nodded and reached into his pocket. He pulled out a locket and handed it to Zhi. She took it and muttered 'thanks' before closing the door.

"Her friend, Arizona, went missing today. I guess, last week, they all went out and Arizona pawned a locket in order to get some money for her brother who is out on the streets. I don't why. Zhi wanted to get it back for her."

"I didn't know she and the missing girl were so close."

Chao shrugged.

"There's a lot to know about Zhi, Miles. A lot."

CHAPTER 7

COME CLEAN

A few weeks went by, and the case hadn't been cracked. Miles was up to her earmuffs in a mess of a case. She had made a little progress thanks to Misty helping her, but it wasn't enough. And the closer that she got without any results, the more Miles drank. She drank with Abby. She drank by herself. She drank with Chao. The only one she didn't have any contact with during the case was Zhi. Oh, she kept tabs on Zhi, but it was only from a distance. Miles just wanted to make sure that she was safe. She did have this pitted feeling in her stomach that she was onto something she wasn't sure she was ready for.

He's out there somewhere. He's out there just waiting to be caught. There haven't been any more deaths. No more cabs picking up women — none of that. He knows we're onto him. He knows his time is limited. We just have to retrace a few more steps and we need a huge clue to really push us over the edge, but this is nearly the end. and I can't wait. Those poor girls are still shaken up. They don't know what to expect or who to talk to and I don't know how to offer my assistance. I need this to be over. I need to be able to know that I can keep these girls safe. I have to.

This was the pep talk that she gave herself each day — well, in between drinks.

The phone rang while she was thinking out loud to herself. It was Misty.

"I'm coming over there."

"Why? What's up?"

"I think I have some information we may have overlooked. You're gonna need some drinks for this one."

"Fine. See you in a few."

Information I may have overlooked?

Miles snorted. She hadn't overlooked any information. In fact, she knew more information than the police knew. She knew from Mr. Slochim that this hadn't been the first time his family had been involved with a kidnapping. She had taken the man's invitation to talk with her about his suspicions.

"I like you. I didn't like you at first. You can understand that my daughter — she is everything."

"I had a father who loved me like that," Miles said. "I would never intentionally hurt her."

"It's more than that. When I was younger, I had a sister that was kidnapped. No ransom. No phone call. They found her body almost two weeks later. The police were looking for a motive, and when they found the man who did it, they asked him why he did it. You want to know what he said?"

"What?"

"He said he had to. He couldn't help himself." Mr. Slochim shook his head. "He was a teacher at her school. He was a friend of the family. We knew him."

"You think you know this guy who tried to take Demi?"

"I know they are looking for a cab driver," Mr. Slochim said. "But you should be looking for someone else — a brother, a son, a someone who has to want these girls."

Miles had appreciated that thought, and it made sense. That was probably why no one had caught this guy. But after a few weeks of scouting through all of the girls who had been kidnapped and learning about the people in their lives, she hadn't nailed him. But Misty said there's missed information?

Or Information she failed to tell me? Or, I don't know, but I know she's been acting hella shady lately. I've been meaning to talk to her, but damn. When she says I might need a drink for this one — she's absolutely correct. I might. In fact, I know I will. So I better prepare myself now. I know this is about to be huge. I know it.

Miles was a little nervous. Not many times did she admitted that she was nervous. Pacing back and forth through the flat, she sipped her bourbon on rocks, contemplating what it is she could have missed. What could it have been?

Misty rushed her way upstairs into the flat throwing the door open.

"What the hell, Misty. I didn't miss anything. I don't miss anything."

Misty nodded and pulled up a chair.

"How many drinks have you had?"

"I'm out of beer, and I'm drinking whiskey."

"Okay. Okay. So, listen, what I'm about to say I need your word that no matter what you won't look at me differently. Don't hold it against me, because if you check my track record, you'll see I've never done anything like this or had any kinda crap like this brought your way."

"Misty!"

"What?"

"You're rambling."

Misty never rambled. When she rambled that meant she was in deep shit.

"So, I started dating a guy seven months ago."

"I knew you were dating Diego!"

"Not him. It was sudden, and I didn't expect it. I wasn't looking for it. I didn't tell you because I didn't think it was a big deal. You know — because I wasn't sure if it would last so why alarm you for no reason?"

"Okay?"

"Well, he's a cab driver…"

"Misty that doesn't mean…"

"Let me finish. He was the same guy that was driving Daniel around. And when you mentioned that you thought you could ask him for help, I got nervous. I was afraid because what if it somehow led you to him? I couldn't live with myself if that were true. So I deflected and tried to make sure you wouldn't talk to him. But the more we've been on this case the more I realize it might be him, and that scares the absolute fuck outta me but I'd rather know than not know."

Miles clenched her teeth together. Misty could see the storm brewing in her eyes.

"So, you thought it would be okay to hide him because he was your boyfriend?"

"No, that's not what I said."

"Oh, that's pretty much the gist of what you said!"

"Dammit, Miles. I didn't think it was him but I didn't want you to start bulldozing his damn house for clues either."

"Yeah, forgive me for doing my damn job and wanting to be there for my best friend. But I guess caring for someone is just too much. Fuck it. It won't happen again."

"Miles! Stop it."

"I'm sorry, but you've never kept secrets from me before. What if he is the guy we're looking for, and you're just letting me look like a crazy person? What if he woulda went after Zhi? How can you even look me in my eyes and ask me not to be upset right now?"

"Miles!"

Miles was just getting started.

"I get it. You aren't sure, but you're suspicious, and

judging by the great work we do, you know damn well when shoes start fitting. You were just being a bitch about it all."

"Because I didn't want you think I was in on it!"

"Why would I ever think that about you? Do you think I don't know you? Don't realize what you're capable of? Like really? By now, you still don't get that I know you?"

"I get it. I just got scared."

The intensity was too much for them. Misty didn't even know what else to say. She knew there was no excuse for not mentioning it to Miles. After all, that was her best friend. Potentially, she could have solved this case a while ago if she were just honest. That was the most infuriating part of all of this. She couldn't even blame Miles for being upset with her. There were serious factors to this pertinent information, and she was harboring what could potentially be a murderer. All because she liked him a lot? It hardly seemed worth it anymore.

Miles had launched into another speech.

"I want you to know what you did is irresponsible as hell. If it were me, you would think I lost my damn mind but because it's you, you want me to sweep it under the rug. I can't in good conscience do that. Maybe you can do something to redeem yourself from this point on. Well, see if you help me catch this guy. You're going to put him behind bars because you owe me and Zhi that much. That girl, Demetria, she's been through hell, and you sit here — in my face, my best damn friend in the universe — telling me you might be dating the dude who tried to rape and kill her? You disgust me right now!"

Misty looked like Miles had punched her in the gut several times. She'd never yelled at Misty before. She'd never cared so much about anyone in her life, but the fact that she felt betrayed weighed heavily on her heart. She didn't know how to directly say it. She wanted to tell Misty so much, but she couldn't get it out any other way — a way Misty would be able to understand because they were destined to be more than friends.

"I know," Misty said. "And I'm gonna fix it. I came to bring you this, but I don't think we need it anymore because I'm more than positive he's the one who did this."

"Then you better make sure that you help me get his ass, 'cause if you don't, I don't see us being friends anymore."

"Can we just…"

"This is hard enough as it is. Let's not until we catch him."

"Okay."

"Is there anything else I need to know? Are there anymore secrets?"

"No. That is all."

Just as Miles was about to tear into her a little bit more, her phone rang. It was a number she didn't recognize, but she still answered. It was part of the job. The part she sometimes hated but sometimes loved; especially when she got a lead. Especially, when it was good news.

"We're on our way!" Miles exclaimed to the other end.

Misty had no idea who it was but it was urgent, and she complied.

I really messed up. I really, really messed up. Miles doesn't have to forgive me. I can't even forgive myself, but I will right this wrong. Giving her the off-grid was one thing, but telling her the truth is another. Even though, it hurts me to know I dropped the ball, I had to. For Arizona— Demetria— Zhi— Miles and every other victim. For my mom... I don't know how other than turning him in, but I'm gonna fix this for sure. I have to. I have to. I HAVE TO. Please let me be able to fix this.

Miles dialed a number when she got into the driver's seat. Misty recognized the voice of Demetria Slochim.

"Hello?" the girl said softly.

"Demi, this is Miles. I want you to tell me exactly what you told the police."

"I just — I was thinking about everything. It's all I can do anymore; think about that day, but I think I might remember where we were initially. And if I can remember that then we can probably..."

"Find Arizona." Misty chimed in.

"Yeah. I mean I know it's a long shot, and I know she's long gone, but I need you to be able to find her. I need her to be at peace. Please."

"If you can remember exactly where you guys were, we can definitely find her. And that can bring us closer to the guy who did this to you."

"I remember his first initial from his cabbie I.D. it was

B. I dunno if it was Brian or Brandon or Brayden, but I remember it ended with an N."

"He didn't even attempt to cover it up?"

"No. Nothing about that ride felt like it would be our last, until it was. Then, it all went by so quick."

"So, it started off pleasant?"

"I remember laying there after we had left Arizona. He was talking to himself. Saying how he couldn't help it and how he had to do this. He said something about protecting his sister. He seemed to be talking in circles."

"Talking in circles?"

"Yeah. He — he would talk about how he had to kidnap us, and then how he had to protect his sister. Then he would get angry and confused about where he was driving. Then he would go by to talking about why he had to do this again." Demi paused. "I remember the alley. There was a dumpster — it was black. Some graffiti. I think it had a devil's horns and a street underneath. I could smell food. It was smoky."

"That's good, Demi. What else do you remember seeing?"

"Gravel everywhere. It wasn't a normal alley — it almost looked — unfinished. He knew where to put her."

"That sounds a lot like Jefferson Alley."

"What?"

"If I take you there right now, do you think you could recognize it?"

"For sure."

"Get ready for us to pick you up."

It was unclear what they would discover when they arrived, but they needed to go. For Arizona. For all of the victims. Because this was much bigger than them. It was much bigger than just a case to solve. This was righting wrongs. This was redemption. This was Misty's chance to figure out how to bring this man in. It wasn't easy, but as soon as they found her it would get easier.

As they drove to Jefferson Alley, it became clearer. This was about to be the breaking point in their case.

<h1 style="text-align:center">CHAPTER 8</h1>

<h2 style="text-align:center">PROTECT AND SERVE</h2>

After finally finding Arizona's body, there was a wave of relief among the girls. Miles put in the call for the coroner and requested an emergency autopsy following the parents identifying the body.

"We need a win here, Miles," O'Neal scratched his head. "I've got the Mayor, the FBI, and more breathing down my neck about the severity of this case."

"I know," Miles sighed.

"No, you don't know. We haven't had a dead body yet. All of the other girls have just not been found. We've got a child murderer as well as a possible rapist and kidnapper. We've got to solve this."

Miles frowned.

"You make it seem like it's more important for us to find her so that we can make everyone happy, Captain.

What about making these girls feel safe again? What about making sure that the years of therapy that they are going to go through isn't going to turn into decades? What about..."

"What about you just do your job," O'Neal snapped. His gaze shifted away from her, down to the ground. She wanted to rip into him. She wasn't one of his men. She didn't obey him. He had no right. Instead, she let him walk away.

They found Arizona's body because of Demetria. So, it was clear that Miles needed some Zhi-time now more than ever. School was about to be released; so, she rushed back to make sure she was there to pick her up. She hadn't talked to her in a while. It had been an awkward run in when Miles and Chao had shown up together that one night. She wasn't sure what she was going to get out of this. She didn't know how she was going to talk to Zhi, but she knew she couldn't avoid it any longer.

She pulled up to the school and waited for Zhi to come out. Hopefully, Zhi wouldn't take this surprise the wrong way. Miles owed it to the kid to spend time with her. They hadn't spent time together since Daniel was caught. Well, since Zhi saw Abby go into Miles' apartment. When Zhi walked out of school, she immediately saw Miles' car. There was a hesitation, and a moment later, several kids came up to Zhi and started talking to her. Miles watched their conversation, but saw Zhi look towards the car several times. Zhi finally broke free from the group and walked to the car. Miles had the door unlocked.

"Come on," she said. "I'll take you home."

"Where the hell have you been, Miles?"

"Trying my damnedest to solve this case."

"Looks like you're doing a great job of that."

"Hey, don't get snarky with me. Just get in."

"No, I'm good. I'll find a ride home."

Miles glared at her.

"Hell, no! Things have changed. Arizona was found dead."

"You don't think I knew that?" Zhi hissed. "All of those girls are dead. It's obvious. And my friends — three are dead. But you're too busy hanging out with my brother and having strange women come into your apartment late at night."

Miles closed her eyes.

"Can you please just get into the car?"

The was nothing for a moment, and then she heard the car down open. Zhi sat back with her arms crossed over her lap. She cleared her throat.

"I already know Arizona's dead, but I would like to be able to say goodbye to my friends the right way. You know, casket and all. Even though I strongly detest funerals."

"How are you though?"

"That has to be the most loaded goddamn question you could ask me right now! Seriously? How am I?"

"It's the right question to ask." Miles says while driving to Foo's.

"I wouldn't say that it is."

"Has anyone else asked you? How are you coping with all of this?"

"I'm not. I'm choosing not to. I don't really even wanna talk about it. My grandpa seems to think I need to, but honestly I've been doing things to take my mind off this."

"You know it's okay to be scared right? You get that it's normal to be afraid of things like this. This was nothing small. Your friends — your inner circle was compromised. Someone was kidnapping your friends."

"I know what was happening! I am well aware! But what I don't understand is why you didn't say something to me sooner than this! I know what you do for a living is important, and I would never expect you to put it on hold but couldn't you have checked on me just once in the last couple of weeks? Was I not important enough for you to protect?"

"Of course you were. It wasn't something I meant to do, I just — I started working harder on this case because of you. Because I needed to catch this guy so that I could put him away. So I could make the streets safe for you. And I realized that in doing that — I didn't even check in. I just kept searching for anything to figure out who he was."

"Yeah, well, do you know who he is? How do you know this guy hasn't been laying low for a while now? If I were gonna do something like this, I would probably get a custom paint job for my car and make sure it was detailed."

"Wait? What?"

"I mean — you guys are looking for a specific cab. I'd change it up. Go off-grid."

"You just might have…"

"You mean, you didn't think of that?"

"I did, but I didn't. Now I definitely need to check into some things. Have any of the girls at school been talking to you?"

"Besides the fact that they are afraid to go anywhere or do anything? Do you know how many are staying home until this psycho is caught? They're even threatening to cancel the school dance because of this shit."

"Well, that wouldn't be the worst thing," Miles muttered. Zhi frowned at her. "I know. Not the point. I've just tried to think of how all of the girls are connected. Maybe there is someone that they all know — someone close. A family member or teacher?"

Zhi shook her head.

"I can't think of anything that connected them all except the fact that they all went to the same school." Zhi leaned her head back against the seat's headrest. "Shit."

It hurt Miles that this was closer to home than she thought it was. Zhi was knew the girls. It was clear they had a good relationship. When they got to the flat, they took off upstairs and Miles grabbed two beers.

"You're almost 18, and you could probably use this right now."

"I've never drank a day in my life."

"Today's a good day to start. It takes the edge off."

"Does it really?"

"Nah, I honestly don't want you to drink, but I figured I needed to offer you something."

"How about a hug?"

"A what?"

"You're such a guy sometimes, Miles."

"Yeah, I guess I can see that."

"Glad you can."

Miles hugged Zhi tightly. She wasn't used to the vulnerability. She didn't like it, but Zhi needed to know someone cared about her and her wellbeing. Chao was a guy. He cared but didn't know how to show it, and Foo was old and couldn't get his emotions together correctly.

"I'm gonna catch the guy who did this to your friends. In fact, I'm almost positive we're close to bringing this thing to the end. I just need you to know. It's okay. I won't ever leave you like that again. I'm sorry. I got caught up trying to get this man. I never knew you were going through all of this. This case was seriously close to home. Your friend Demi — she's the hero in all of this. I promise you it's all gonna come to a head soon."

"You know when Demi came to me and told me what happened, I was so scared. I thought about you and my grandfather and Chao, but then I thought about Ari and her girlfriend, Violet, and how she must be feeling right now. Her girlfriend just disappeared. She just disappeared and was found dead."

Miles walked through to the kitchen to grab a glass so

she could start in on the cognac. She needed something stronger than the beer. This was all too much, too suddenly. This whole story was more involved than she thought. It was a story of love and loss of finding yourself of betrayal. She couldn't even fathom it. She chugged the cognac and poured another glass. When she came back to the table she was riddled with confusion.

"Wait. Who is Violet?"

"She's Ari's girlfriend. It's kind of on the DL. Ari's parents would have thrown a fit if they knew she liked girls. So, Ari and Vi didn't make it public. Only a few of us knew. Vi's been going through a super hard time since all of this happened. She can't even process things at home because her mom is like super religious. Super religious. So, she's been left to grieve without the strength of her family. She's only got, well, me now."

"I thought maybe Demetria and Arizona maybe, but I didn't even know there was a whole different piece to this puzzle."

"Demi and Ari are best friends. They used to be more a few years ago but that faded out. So now, it's Ari and Vi. Well — it was."

"And now Vi is all alone, and so is Demi."

"Yeah. Demi still loved Ari though."

"You don't think Demi could have..."

"Had something to do with this? No! Never! Demi loved Ari so much. They were best friends. She loved everything about her. She would never want anything bad to happen to her. At all."

"Yeah, but something bad did happen to her, and Demi got out of it. You ever ask yourself why? How did she escape when the others didn't? How come she got away?"

"The guy got sloppy. Trust me, Miles. It's not her. Demi would never hurt anyone in this world! Especially not Ari."

"You said they dated before? Demi still had feelings for Ari?"

"She did, but have you met Demi's parents? They would never be on board with that. Never in a million years."

"Okay, but what if Demi's parents had something to do with it? What if they hired someone to get rid of Ari because they found out about their relationship?"

"Why would they do that? Why would they put their own daughter through that?"

"People are crazy."

"Demi's parents have a lot of money. I mean, an insane amount. They could hire anyone to do anything. But I just don't see it. I don't think anyone would want to hurt their own child like that."

"What do you mean like that?"

"You ever feel like you can't breathe because the one thing that was worth it was taken from you?"

Miles looked down at the beer in her hand. She felt that way about Misty at the moment.

"Demi hides it well."

"Too well."

"Yes."

"She's not coping any better than Vi is."

Teenagers were a mess. Teenagers were never this confusing when she was growing up. Or maybe she was just out of touch with it all.

"So let me get this straight. Demi was in love with Ari, but they couldn't be together because Demi's parents would have a fit. Yet, Vi's mom is super religious, but Vi didn't care about that as long as she could be with Ari. And in the midst of all of this, Ari and Demi were together in that cab. Granted they didn't do anything, but who is to say they didn't think about it. So now Vi not only has to think about the fact Ari isn't coming back but…"

"But she had to think about the fact that her girlfriend was with her ex right before she died."

"This is brutal."

"You should know," Zhi said. Miles looked at her.

"What are you talking about?"

"That girl — the one I saw the night Daniel got arrested — who was she?"

"Just a friend, Zhi."

"A friend that spends the night — a lot." Miles could see the questioning in her eyes. "I don't judge, Miles. If you're — you know — a lesbian, then that's cool. I just — I thought that…"

"What?"

Zhi shrugged.

"I thought you would tell me."

Miles could see that Zhi was hurt. The girl considered Miles a sister and close friend.

"It's not like that, Zhi. I—I haven't told anyone. It's not easy. You've seen that with your friends."

"Yeah, but even though it was tough, and even with all of the drama, we've been there for each other. You're not letting anyone in."

Miles wanted to dismiss what Zhi was saying. She was just a teenager. She was right though. Miles was tired of keeping the secret. It kind of felt good that someone else knew — someone other than Abby.

"So, do you love this girl?" Zhi asked. "Tell me about her."

"Oh, boy," Miles rolled her eyes. "We will talk about this some other time. You've got homework, I'm sure, and I need to get this case solved."

Zhi walked over and hugged Miles.

"I know you will. Thank you."

CHAPTER 9

He hadn't picked up his sister in a while. He honestly didn't want to draw attention to himself. This would be the first time he picked her up in his cab since it got repainted. He was kind of excited to see what she thought of the cab.

"I almost didn't recognize you! When did you do this?"

"I think I did it right after all the craziness started."

"But why?"

"I didn't want them thinking it was me. I figured if I changed things up, they'd know it couldn't have been me."

"But it already wasn't you though."

"I know, but I wanted to stand out from the crowd. These guys would have gotten it all wrong. Probably wanted to search all in my shit which is a damn headache."

"But why would you care anyway? I mean, I don't get it."

"You and I both know I'm not the most legit person. Who knows what they would have found: guns, drugs, whatever. You know what I do, so I don't know why you would even ask me."

"I'm just saying, you might have ruined your chances of being in the clear. They're calling for all cabs to be searched, and you turn around and do this? You made yourself hot for doing this stupid shit."

"Vi, don't even act like you know what this life is like."

"Don't act like I don't remember who got you into this shit either."

"We don't talk about him."

"You mean your real father?"

"Shut up, Vi. He's just a sperm donor, and you know it."

"He's the guy who set you up to fail. You were doing good for yourself until he came around and told you the truth. Now, look at you. All because of George; your fuckin' sperm donor."

"Stop talking about him. Damn. He's looked out the last couple times."

"Yea, at whose expense though? Remember that guy you were driving around? He ended up in the feds, and I can't promise that you won't either. George is fucking dangerous. You don't get it. He's gonna keep using you, and you're gonna keep allowing it, and I can't sit and watch this shit anymore. I stay silent but, dammit, you're being stupid!"

They never talked about George. George was his

biological father, but he couldn't stand talking about him. He wasn't the best role model. Violet's dad, the war hero, was his father in his heart. George was the man who helped him out whenever he was in a jam. Anytime. But that's really all he was good for. He wasn't the kind of person to give you sound advice or a hug or tell you everything would be okay. He just equated every problem to money. It was funny because he had plenty of it and plenty of problems because of it.

"How do you think I can afford the things we have? You think that money just falls in my lap? I hustle so you don't have to. You forget you're gonna go to college this summer? You think that shit is free?"

"It is. I have a scholarship. So don't you dare shift the blame on me; not for your fucked-up ways. I won't allow it. I've been busting my damn ass to make sure I don't have to live here forever; to make sure I don't end up just the little sister of a dope lord. I guess it's true what they say. Like father, like son."

"You don't get to pretend you haven't reaped every benefit from this dope money. You don't get to lecture me like you know the things I've sacrificed or been through to keep you outta these streets. I would kill people so you can live. I pushed a little stuff, but I never actually sold anything. I just make sure it gets to its destination. That's it. But yes. I have had to lay some people out. No, I'm not proud of it, but if it's them or me. It's always gonna be them."

She couldn't even say anything. Her brother became someone she didn't even recognize anymore. He was some tough-talkin' thug like the ones he warned her to stay away from, the ones she knew better than to get involved in, and the ones that could get you killed being at the wrong place at the wrong time.

"Fine."

"Throw your backpack in the backseat. I got something I need to put up in the front with us before we get home."

"If this is a run, I swear to God…"

"Keep your damn mouth shut. I have this. You just shut up and be quiet."

He pulled up to an alley and jumped out of the car. She couldn't even believe he would bring her somewhere dangerous. She didn't know where she was, but she knew Jefferson Alley wasn't too far from there. Jefferson Alley; where they just found the love of her life dead. Jefferson Alley; where they used to meet secretly to kiss or just hold hands. Jefferson Alley, where their lives together ended. He hurried back to the car with something in his coat.

"What the fuck?"

"I thought you might need someone to keep you company."

In his coat was a 6-week-old golden retriever. He bought the dog for her earlier thinking it may help her cope. He felt guilty enough as it was. He didn't know, and now that he did, he was trying everything to not allow it to eat him up.

"OHHHHHH MY GOOODDDDDDDDD!!!! A PUPPYYYYY! What's his name?"

"You name him. He's yours."

"Can — can I name him Ari?"

"I would hope that you would."

"Good because that's what I wanna name him."

"Then that's his name."

"Thank you! So much!"

The puppy was anxiously jumping between the two of them in the cab. Happy to be around them. He licked Vi's face, and she lit up like he'd never seen before. He did right. He never meant to hurt her ever. His sister was his whole world. He'd do anything for her. Anything at all.

He drove her home, and they got settled in. He got a phone call from George, but decided to ignore it. He was bothered by all of this. He decided he needed some air. He jumped in his mustang and just began driving.

I don't know where I'm going. I don't care. I just needed to get away. This pain that I've caused Violet — I don't even know how to fix this. How can I? I can't. I wouldn't forgive me. I wouldn't. I don't. George might know what to do. I should probably call him back. I don't even know.

I hurt my fucking sister. I killed the love of her life. I killed her. Things just got so outta hand. Shut up, stop thinking about it. You didn't mean it. Yes, you did. No, you didn't. Yes, you did. You meant it. You did those other girls. You just didn't think it would hurt someone you loved as well. Now look at you — buying puppies to ease the pain you caused. You're outta control.

You should just kill yourself before they figure it out. They're gonna figure it out you know? And guess what? When they do, Vi will know, and she'll hate you. She'll hate you more than you ever thought anyone could hate you. She'll hate you more than you hated George when you found out he was your real father. She'll hate you more than you hate yourself. And she'll be well within her rights. You killed a piece of her. Get yourself together. There's no time for pity parties. You're riding around with all of this guilt right now. Because you fucked up. As usual. You fucked up. You fucked up big time.

He knew what he needed to do. So, he did exactly that. He pulled into the familiar parking lot and got out of his car. He made his way in and got himself comfortable in the booth.

"Forgive me, Father, for I have sinned. It's been 5 years since my last confession."

"What is it, my son?"

"Father, I have broken one of the ten commandments. Repeatedly."

"Continue, my child."

"I hurt people, Father. I hurt them badly. I don't want to keep hurting them, so I came here to ask for forgiveness. I know that you can't tell anyone what we discuss, but Father, I don't wish to say too much. God knows that I have sinned. He has seen all that I've done and I can assure you — he is displeased. I need to be forgiven, Father — the weight of the guilt is so heavy."

"How many times did you break the commandment my child?"

"More than a dozen."

"You should say 72 Hail Marys and fast for a week's time. Pray with me; your act of contrition as I absolve your sin."

"Bless you, Father."

"God, the Father of mercies, through the death and resurrection of his Son has reconciled the world to himself and sent the Holy Spirit among us for the forgiveness of sins; through the ministry of the Church may God give you pardon and peace, and I absolve you from your sins in the name of the Father, and of the Son, and of the Holy Spirit."

"Oh my God, I am heartily sorry for having offended Thee, and I detest all my sins because of Thy just punishments, but most of all because they offend Thee, my God, Who art all-good and deserving of all my love. I firmly resolve, with the help of Thy grace, to sin no more and to avoid the near occasions of sin."

As he left the confessional, he went to his pew and silently prayed his Hail Marys. 72 in a row. It took him a while to complete the task, but he felt better. For someone who didn't believe anymore, he still practiced basic principles like praying when things didn't feel right. He didn't even know who he was praying to. Was it really God? He didn't know. He didn't care. His conscience was a little clearer now that he finally told someone what he did. He knew he didn't have to go into detail. He was smart enough not to, but his luck was running out. He knew it was coming to a close, but he still kept trying. Foolish. He thought about just turning himself in. It would be easier than pretending he had no idea, but he knew he was foolish. Arrogant even.

CHAPTER 10

VIOLET

She forgot she left her bag in the back of the cab. She had a few assignments to finish. The craziest thing about all of this was she maintained her good grades the entire time. When she went to the back, she accidentally hit the seat and a ring fell from the seat. She had one on her ring finger exactly like it. She and Ari had bought each other matching rings as a symbol of their love. She had it inscribed with her name and their date. Something overcame her with anxiety. She knew it wasn't Ari's, but she just had to look anyway. And what she found made her sick to her stomach. The inscription proved otherwise. That was Ari's ring. Ari had been in her brother's cab. It all started to make sense – him getting his cab redone from the interior to the paint job, him not coming home, him not reacting when she told him about her girlfriend. Her brother was a murderer. Until now, she didn't necessarily see him as a terrible person, but now the shoe was on the other foot.

There has to be some kinda explanation for this. Think Vi. Think. He didn't kill her, did he? Did he? How could he? I mean what would the purpose be? Why would he kill her? Ari, what did you do, baby? Did he — I don't wanna think about it. I can't think about it. What can I do? My brother? He's the psycho. Or is he covering up for George? I don't know what to do. I don't know. I don't know. I don't know. Wait — what was that P.I.'s name? The one that's been working with Demi? Think Vi. Think. Call Demi.

She grabbed her phone and dialed Demetria's number.

"Hey."

"Hey, listen — that detective you've been talking to — what's her information?"

"Why?"

"I think I might have a lead on something."

"How could you? You weren't even there. How could you have something?"

"Just give me the info. Please."

"I'll text it to you right now. Call Zhi afterwards, too. I think she knows the P.I."

"Does she?"

"Yeah. I think she's a friend of the family. Just — if you know something — make it good. Please."

"I will."

She hung up the phone and waited for the text. She thought she should wait until he came home so she could ask him, but everything in her gut told her she should just turn him in. He was the one. He did it. And what's worse? He did it to her girlfriend. He messed with the wrong girl. He messed with his sister. And she was in no mood to forgive him for what he did. Ever.

When he finally arrived home, she was still there waiting for him. She hadn't called yet. She couldn't. She had to hear his side of the story first. Vi knew it would hurt her even more but she had to know why. Why? What would make him do this?

"I know." She said firmly. She didn't even want to start that way, but she did.

"Know what?" he asked, oblivious to whatever she was talking about.

"I had to get my backpack out of the car; so, I had to get to the backseat. When I asked you why you got everything redone? You said that you wanted it to set you apart from the others. It did. But there's something you overlooked. You see this? This ring I've been wearing for the last 7 months? My girlfriend had one that was matching. I bought it for her because I needed her to wear a symbol of my love every day. You — you didn't bank on her dropping her ring in the back of your cab, though. You didn't bank on me going to the back and finding it, and you didn't bank on me looking for the inscription to confirm my suspicions. You killed my heart and soul. You looked me right in my face, and you acted hurt when you found out about my girlfriend. All the while you killed her! You!"

"I didn't even know — I didn't kill her. Okay? I didn't. She was already — she, like, passed out before I could even — I just left her there in Jefferson Alley. I didn't kill her. I swear."

"You kidnapped her and you killed her! You buy me a damn puppy to make up for killing my girlfriend! That's supposed to make it better? You kept promising me I was safe! I was safe! My friends should have been safe too! You…"

"Shut up! Don't say another fuckin word! I don't wanna hear it. I can't. Just stop talking!"

"Oh no! You owe me every fuckin' detail. Every damn detail from the time you picked her up 'til the time you dropped her off. I wanna know and you need to tell me!"

"I didn't know you knew her."

"You don't know who I know!"

The tension between the two was so thick you could cut it with a butcher's knife. She was right. He didn't know who she knew. And now that he knew a little, he felt sick to his stomach.

"You're right. I don't. And if I would've known, I swear I would have never…"

"You shouldn't have either way! The rest of them was that you too? Or what?"

"They were ordered."

"Ordered for who?"

"I look I can't talk about it."

"You better start fuckin' talking right now."

"I was doing a job for a guy and things just got outta hand. We were just supposed to — look I'd never hurt you on purpose, Vi. You know that."

"I don't think I can ever forgive you. Ever."

"I don't expect you to. I don't expect anything from you at all. I took something from you. Something you'll never get back. Love."

"You took the one thing in this world that mean everything to me. You, my brother of all people, and you won't even tell me why…"

"It won't help when I say it."

"How do you know? You won't even…"

"I'm sorry. Okay? I wish like hell I could tell you but I can't. This shit got way too deep, and I don't know…"

"You messed up though. You left Demi alive…"

"You know that girl too?"

"Demi and Ari were best friends because they couldn't be together anymore. You went after them not knowing they were my friends. My friends. And I loved them so much. I loved them more than I ever loved anyone, and to see Demi so hurt and know that you had something to do with it? You killed more than my girlfriend. You killed me. My heart. My trust. My loyalty to you. You killed me."

He's a damn coward. My brother is a coward. He killed her.

He literally killed my girlfriend. I can't even stand the sight of this man anymore. How could he just — take a life like that? What would I do if it were just a regular girl and not my girlfriend? Would I still be as enraged? I want to say yes, but really, I can't say it would be equal. I'd be lying. But those other girls were important too. They don't even mention them anymore. Everything on the news has been about Ari and Demi — because Demi survived, I guess? My brother is a GODDAMN COWARD.

"How can I make it right?"

"Turn yourself in."

She handed him the phone. He looked at her shocked at her suggestion, but she was serious. He couldn't even believe it.

"You gotta be shittin' me. I'd never get outta prison. They'd give me lethal injection. I can't do that. Are you serious?"

"You seriously killed my girlfriend."

"I — seriously — had no idea who she was."

"And that seriously doesn't make it any fuckin' better!"

"Stop yelling at me! Please!"

"What would you do if you were me? Think about me for once in this whole thing! You took her from me! You took her! And now you want me to feel sorry for you."

"Pray with me."

"What?"

"I need you to pray with me."

"I can't even…"

"Please."
"You don't even believe in prayer."
"Pray with me."
"I want to, but — you're too far gone."
She walked away.

CHAPTER 11

CLOSING IN

Misty's fingers danced around the phone sitting on the table in front of her. She needed a drink. Too bad there were no damn beers in the fridge. This was the moment that she wished she were more like Miles.

Come on, Misty. Suck it up.

She grabbed the phone and dialed. He picked up on the first ring.

"What!" The anger in his voice charged through the phone like a bull. She jumped a little and was thankful that no one was there to witness that.

"What are you up to?"

"I — just got into the house."

"Do you wanna meet me somewhere?"

"Yeah. I could use some air."

"You could?"

"Yeah. It's been rough over here. I don't even know — I just need to get out. Can I come see you?"

"I definitely want you to."

"Well, then, I'm on my way."

"Great."

Misty practically dropped the phone and shook her hands in the air.

"Okay, Misty. Deep breaths. You've got this."

She was about to set him up. She was trapping this man. She knew without a doubt he was the killer. This was her righting her wrong. She grabbed the phone and called Miles.

"So, you told Zhi about it. How do you feel?"

Miles snorted as she and Abby sat down in her apartment over food.

"That was a very therapist thing to say. You're getting better at it."

Abby smirked.

"Avoiding the question."

Miles rolled her eyes and shrugged. "I mean, she's just a kid. I don't know if I should bring her into my world."

"She is a part of your world though, isn't she? Doesn't your case prove that? You can't keep the world from getting to Zhi."

"So, how do I protect her?"

"You mean, how do you protect yourself?"

"Damn you." Miles shoved a forkful of food in her

mouth. Abby had really become her therapist. Sure, there was some sex sprinkled in there, but Miles felt like their relationship was very one-sided in that department. Abby knew things — a lot of things.

"So, Misty," Abby said. "When is that going to happen?"

"I'm having some trust issues with Misty right now. I'm not sure what I'm going to..." At that moment, Miles' phone rang. She sighed. "Speak of the devil herself."

"I think I have a lead." Misty said when Miles picked up.

"What?"

"I invited him over. He's not gonna tell me the truth, but if he's here, you can make sure he doesn't leave. You can get him."

"Misty, are you crazy? You can't meet up with him. No."

"Too late. Miles, I've got this. Just let the police know he's our man and get them at my apartment, ready for my signal."

She hung up the phone, and Miles growled as she squeezed it into her hands. Abby set down her fork and grabbed a napkin.

"You need to go, huh?"

"Yeah, I do. This is why I should work alone."

The door to Miles' apartment swung open, and Zhi ran in with a wild-eyed look on her face.

"Miles! I..." She stopped when she saw Abby.

"Zhi," Miles snapped her fingers, and the girl returned her focus.

"My friend, Violet just called me! It's about her brother! She thinks he's the killer!"

"Why does she think this?"

"She said she found evidence in his cab that he killed her. She said she wanted him to be taken in and arrested, but she didn't want him to realize that she turned him in."

"And he's headed over to Misty's now," Miles groaned. "Zhi texted me your friend's number! I'm going over there."

"I'm coming, too!" Zhi exclaimed.

"Hell, no. You stay far away from this."

"But…"

Abby cleared her throat.

"Zhi, I'm Abby. Heard a lot about you. I'll stay with you here if you want. I can be a good friend."

Zhi didn't look at Abby. Her eyes stayed on Miles, and it was like there was a silent communication between them. Zhi finally nodded, and Miles left.

Abby stood up from her chair and walked over to the girl. There were no words as she wrapped her arms around Zhi, and after a few seconds, Zhi relaxed into the hug and cried.

PRAYER CIRCLE

"*Our Father, which art in heaven,*
Hallowed be thy Name.
Thy Kingdom come.
Thy will be done in earth,
As it is in heaven.
Give us this day our daily bread.
And forgive us our trespasses,
As we forgive them that trespass against us.
And lead us not into temptation,
But deliver us from evil.
For thine is the kingdom,
The power, and the glory,
For ever and ever.
Amen."

He'd said that prayer a million times in his life. He

stopped praying because he knew he was a monster. He knew he was no good. But now everything changed. He come clean to his sister even though it was the hardest thing he ever had to do. The craziest part was he kept thinking to just end it all. He thought to just commit suicide and end the suffering of everyone around him, but he was too cowardly. He was used to quoting scriptures. His mother would be ashamed of him. His sister already was. He knew he couldn't tell his girlfriend. He knew he had to keep it to himself, but part of him needed to feel a release.

He called Misty from his car.

"Would you be mad if—"

"If you canceled on me at the last minute?"

"No. If I asked you to come to my car, like, just to talk?"

"Umm… yeah, that's fine."

"Great. I'm downstairs right now. It's kinda chilly out here, so, bundle up?"

"Yeah. I will."

She texted Miles quickly and headed downstairs.

"Hey."

"Hey."

"I'm sorry I just showed up like this it's just a lot going on. I got into it with someone I really care about and nothing made any sense. So, I figured I would come to the person who else helped me make sense out of everything."

"What do you need me to do?"

"I — this is gonna sound crazy. Are you a praying woman?"

"Not at all."

"Do you at least believe in some kind of higher power?"

"Yes."

"I made some mistakes, and I don't think I'll ever be able to make amends to those mistakes."

"What do you mean?"

"I fucked up."

"How?"

"I can't tell you."

"Okay. I won't force you. I'm just saying eventually you'll need to release, and when you're ready, I'll be here too."

"There was this girl, she — I dunno — I think — Never mind."

"A girl?"

"A girl — that used to care about me — and I think I might have hurt her. By not wanting to be with her."

"Oh. Listen, I'm not a praying woman. Mainly because when my parents were still in my life, they forced me to pray for hours at a time. Forced me to believe that some superior God was coming to save me from all of my problems. He never did. That God they promised me would come save me from poverty and hunger and depression never showed up. So it was finally when I was 15 that I didn't believe in it anymore. Then I lost my dad, and I thought if God was real that was probably him punishing me. So, I don't pray anymore. I can't. Because I'm all out of owed favors from God. He doesn't owe me anything. And in return, I don't ask for anything."

"What's the most horrible thing you've ever done in your life?" he asked.

"I couldn't even tell you," she replied.

"Because you've never done anything?" he countered.

"Because I've done enough," she hissed.

"What constitutes as enough?" he inquired.

"More than we can talk about in one car sitting," she said.

"There's these scriptures that I recite sometimes." He hesitated.

"Oh?" She raised her eyebrows.

"Yea. Psalms is like my favorite book of the Bible." He smiled.

"Why is that?" She questioned.

"It's the most relative." He shrugged.

"Oh?"

"Though my father and mother forsake me, the Lord will receive me. Teach me your way, Lord; lead me in a straight path because of my oppressors. Do not turn me over to the desire of my foes, for false witnesses rise up against me, spouting malicious accusations. I remain confident of this: I will see the goodness of the Lord —in the land of the living. Wait for the Lord; be strong and take heart and wait for the Lord."

"Psalms 27: 10 through 14."

"You may not be a praying woman anymore, but the word is still the word. And you still know it's the word."

"Wanna know my favorite scripture?"

"Yes."

"If anyone has caused grief, he has not so much grieved me as he has grieved all of you to some extent—not to put it too severely. The punishment inflicted on him by the majority is sufficient. Now instead, you ought to forgive and comfort him, so that he will not be overwhelmed by excessive sorrow. I urge you, therefore, to reaffirm your love for him. Another reason I wrote you was to see if you would stand the test and be obedient in everything. Anyone you forgive, I also forgive. And what I have forgiven—if there was anything to forgive—I have forgiven in the sight of Christ for your sake, in order that Satan might not outwit us. For we are not unaware of his schemes."

"Second Corinthians."

"Yea. I may not be a praying woman, but it's still in me. I don't mean to come across as rude when you talk to me about your faith. I once believed as you did. I just eventually — stopped believing in all of it, and focused on the truth."

"You know how Saul was — all bad?"

"Yea."

"What if I'm him?"

He was every bit of Saul. The only difference was that Saul redeemed himself.

CHAPTER 13

ALL HEROES DON'T WEAR CAPES

There he was in all his glory. Sitting in the car next to her best friend. He looked troubled. It made no sense how calm they were. Miles had no idea what to do. She was getting ready to close in on the car, and this guy was getting ready to probably spill his entire heart out to her best friend.

"C'mon, Misty. I'm about to take this fucker down." She mumbled to herself— hoping Misty would know better. "Get out of the way Misty. I'm about to take his ass out."

She called for backup just in case. This was about to be something serious. It was too risky not to call. Too risky for everyone involved — especially Misty. She was still upset at that part. Misty didn't do things like this. She didn't put herself in danger. That was Miles' job. Now, she was in a confined area with a fuckin' killer.

"I need you to get here, Captain! I'm going in, and I could sure use your help. We got our guy. I need you here, but don't draw any attention to yourself. Get here!"

"We will get there, Miles. You just hold on."

"Hold on! I swear if you blow this…"

"Miles. Don't screw it up 'cause you're close to this. We're on our way. Hang tight. It may take a few minutes."

"Yea."

It took precisely a few minutes before they got to the scene.

This kid doesn't even know his own sister ratted on him. She needed to. He's a severe danger to himself. I drank so damn much, my head is pounding. My heart is throbbing through my chest. It's go time. We're about to apprehend the perp. This is for Ari, for Cami, for Demi, for Stacy — and their families. I wonder if there were more? There very well could be. This is for them, too.

"Miles, we got here as soon as we could. You're positive this is the guy?" Captain O'Neal asked softly.

"I just got confirmation from his little sister that it was him. Apparently, the guy killed his own little sister's girlfriend. She found her ring inside his cab — a cab which he had repainted. A cab, he made sure no one saw the last couple of weeks, and he was smart enough to do it. He was smart enough to make everything disappear — except that."

"You ready to go in?"

"I'm as ready as I'll ever be!"

"Let's get this thing going then — on my signal."

Misty saw the movement out of the corner of her eye. She knew time was up. Boston had poured his heart out, and while she could see that there was a struggle in his soul, she couldn't help him. It was too late.

"I'm so sorry," Misty choked back the tears. Boston looked at her. She swallowed hard and closed her eyes. She didn't want to see it happen. "I hope you find the God you're looking for."

At that moment, the cops burst into the scene, guns drawn and their cuffs ready.

"Get your ass out of the car now!"

"What's happening?" Boston screamed.

"Boston! Get out of the car! Now!"

"Wait! No!"

Misty kept her eyes closed.

"Don't reach for the gun, I know you have," she said. "Boston, please, don't fight this. I promise you that this is what you need."

"Misty! No! Look at me!" She felt his hands grab for her. She grabbed onto the door handle. She could hear the officers yelling, the driver's door being forced open, Boston yelling and being dragged out of the car.

"You have the right to remain silent. Anything you say can and will be used against you in a court of law. You have the right to an attorney. If you cannot afford an attorney, one will be provided for you. Do you understand the rights I have just read to you? With these rights in mind, do you wish to speak to me?"

"You can't do this! I haven't done anything!"

"You're under arrest for the murder of Arizona Wahlberg."

"You've gotta be joking me, right now!"

"Are you waiving your rights?"

Boston started to mumble to himself.

"Whoever dwells in the shelter of the Most High will rest in the shadow of the Almighty. I will say of the Lord, "He is my refuge and my fortress, my God, in whom I trust." Surely he will save you from the fowler's snare and from the deadly pestilence. He will cover you with his feathers, and under his wings you will find refuge; his faithfulness will be your shield and rampart. You will not fear the terror of night, nor the arrow that flies by day, nor the pestilence that stalks in the darkness, nor the plague that destroys at midday. A thousand may fall at your side, ten thousand at your right hand, but it will not come near you. You will only observe with your eyes and see the punishment of the wicked. if you say, "The Lord is my refuge," and you make the Most High your dwelling, no harm will overtake you, no disaster will come near your tent. For he will command his angels concerning you to guard you in all your ways; they will lift you up in their hands, so that you will not strike your foot against a stone."

They cuffed him and placed him into the back of a squad car.

Miles ran up to the car and threw open the passenger's door.

"What the fuck! Misty, what the hell were you thinking!"

"Miles, I'm okay," Misty said getting out of the car. Miles wasn't listening thought.

"I don't care! What wrong with you. You lie to me. You sneak around with information. You pull this stupid move that could have gotten you killed. Why?"

"I'm sorry, Miles," Misty pleaded. She hugged her arms around her chest and looked down to the ground. "I'm sorry, I hurt you."

"Hurt me? Hurt me! You have no fuckin' clue!"

"Clue about what?"

Miles grabbed Misty by the shoulders and shook her. It happened before she knew it. She wasn't sure who was shocked more — her or Misty. When they kissed though, Miles was afraid to stop. She was afraid to let go. It felt better than her dreams and imagination. She wanted to cry and laugh. She wanted to stay in that moment; afraid of what would happen when it ended.

Misty's eyes were wide when Miles took a step back. For a moment, there was silence. Miles took a step back as Misty placed her fingers on her lips to see if they really felt what they did.

"I, uh, um," Miles fumbled. Misty gulped loudly.

"Miles?"

Miles couldn't stay there. She turned and ran through the oblivious officers on the scene and took off in her car.

CHAPTER 14

HARD DECISIONS

Turning Boston in was the hardest thing she had ever had to do. She wrestled with it for a while before she finally did what she needed to do. There was still more unfinished business she had for the person who hired Ari's killer. He had no idea it was coming, and she planned to keep it that way. As far as Boston was concerned, she didn't even flinch when they took him away. He killed the love of her life. That kind of pain was something you don't get over easily if at all. She was determined to administer the same pain she was feeling. An eye for an eye, as far as she was concerned.

Now that Boston was captured, that left her to make sure her mother was taken care of. It was unfair— but it was life. Everyone they loved was now gone. Her father and now her brother. She still couldn't believe he killed her girlfriend. She missed Ari more than she knew what to do with. At times it was unbearable. The closeness they shared, the secrets — he didn't just kill her girlfriend, he killed her best friend.

She had to go back to school and face everyone, including Demetria. She didn't even know how to face her. She felt so bad.

"So, your brother?"

"My brother."

"I thought my family was fucked up."

"I guess we just never know what people are going through."

"I guess not. It had to be hard, turning him in — I mean, it was your brother."

"But she was my girlfriend, and you are my friend. Wrong is wrong."

"Yeah. I thought maybe I would see you and want to beat your face in — you know, 'cause part of me wanted to blame you."

"So, you're not blaming me?"

"How could I? How could I even think to blame you for what your brother did? You lost the love of your life. You wouldn't even — no, I'm not mad at you. You had to do something so hard, and you did it in the name of love. You stood up for me. You helped me and for that I appreciate you."

"You know I didn't do anything that major right? He needed to be turned in. He hurt her."

"And those other girls."

"And you."

"I was more afraid because I didn't think I would get away. I just knew for sure I was gonna be the next girl who was held captive. I'm sorry. I know that's your brother. How are you even coping with all of this?"

"What other choice do I have? I don't wanna play victim. That takes away from you and Ari — who actually paid with her life."

"She tried, you know, to be a hero. She—"

"I know. I just wish it didn't have to be this way. It's hard enough to live in this world — to be gay in this world. Hell, to be a girl in this world. But the fact that he was my brother, and that he WOULD do something to her — to you, to any other girl — is what keeps playing back in my head."

"You couldn't stop it, though. You didn't even know, and when you found out, you did what you had to do; so, you're essentially a hero."

"I feel less than super right now."

"I would say that comes with the territory. I don't know, but I know everyone else is mad at you for things beyond your control, and here I am proud of you. We all have choices. I think it's interesting that everyone is talking shit, but they wouldn't have known what to do if they were faced with the same situation."

"How long do I have to pretend I'm okay before I'm allowed to fall apart?"

"I'd say whenever you're ready, my shoulder is available."

"Promise?"

"Promise."

She wasn't ready just yet, but it felt good to know that when she was, she at least had one friend who understood her enough to be there.

People take things like that for granted. Being there. Listening. Consoling. It's all necessary. After all of this, she knew she was due for couch time. She wasn't quite ready to share her story though. Boston, her kind-hearted brother, who would literally give anyone the shirt off his back, had killed people for money, for acceptance, for his own demons, and it made her sick to her stomach.

She walked herself to class, just thinking about the last time she'd seen Arizona. It was in the bathroom right before English class. They shared the softest kiss and told each other they loved each other. Then they walked hand in hand to class. They were happy. Nothing could have torn them apart. Until, Boston ruined it all.

He ruined her trust in people, her faith and belief in love, he ruined her plans for the future. Her whole life was a lie.

You really outdid yourself, you bastard. You really did. You took everything from me — you, my girlfriend, my sanity. But if I had to do it all over again, I'd turn you in twice. Mama — Mama will forgive you, but me? I won't. I don't see the reason. You lied to me. You hurt people, and you lied. You ruined families. You had the whole city upset. Boston, you bastard, you ain't never been no good ever since you found George again. Well, he's got it coming to him — he better hope and pray I don't ever come in contact with him again.

"Violet?"

"Yes?"

"You know, no matter what, everything is gonna be okay, right?" Zhi said to her while they settled into class.

"Yes."

"Good, because sometimes life really sucks but that doesn't mean it won't get better."

"You sound like an after-school special."

"Sorry."

"I appreciate you, Zhi."

"Listen, don't go all gay on me," Zhi joked.

Suddenly, she smiled a genuine smile, and she realized everything was indeed okay.

Want Free Books?

Join my newsletter to receive updates on my new book releases go to my website at purplepress.org to sign up.

Join My Newsletter

Reviews are essential to my growth. If you enjoyed this book, I would love it if you took a moment to leave a honest review. A few sentences is plenty, just enough to let fellow readers know what you liked about this book.

Thank you in advance, we appreciate and couldn't do this without you.

For more information:
purplepress.org
PurplePressLLC@gmail.com

Dylan Keefer is a web designer / developer by day and a writer by night. He's basically a modern day superhero, using code and words to breathe creativity into reality. On a more serious note, he has been writing from a very young age and has always been pursuing the dream of writing professionally. Everything he does is in pursuit of that dream. He writes light-hearted as well as dark themed stories across multiple genres. His stories involve psychological struggles or moral dilemmas of the human condition. If you like those themes and the idea of questioning what it means to be human, then it won't matter what genre the story is; he will make you a believer.

Series

The Blood Rite Saga

The Blood Empire: Episode One

The Blood Princess: Episode One

The Blood Princess: Episode Two

The Blood Princess: Episode Three

The Blood Princess: Episode Four

The Blood Princess: Episode Five

The Chronicles of Gandos

The Sword of Light

The Aurora Chronicles

Child of Winter

Lake of Prophecy

Taste of Battle

Heart of Will

Spirits of Arktika

The Raine Michelson Files

Angel's Poison

Demon's Match

Satan's Torment

Devil's Advocate

Lucifer's Wake

Mischief Miles Investigations

A Familiar Scent

Breaking and Entering

Like Father, Like Son

Too Close For Comfort

Mr. Right or Mr. Wrong

Everscape Online

Traitor of Golden Blaze

Queen of Ragnarok

Champion of Everscape

Britney Allen: The London Crime Syndicate

Blood of Babes: The Slasher Files

Standalone

Lost in Space

The Lone Survivor

Mr. Buddy Bot

Evelyn